MOVEMENT

OTHER BOOKS
by
Valerie Miner

Murder in the English Department, a novel, St. Martin's Press, New York, 1982, The Women's Press, London, 1982

Blood Sisters, a novel, The Women's Press, London, 1981, St. Martin's Press, New York, 1982

Co-Author:

Tales I Tell My Mother, short stories, South End Press, Boston, 1980

Her Own Woman, journalism, Macmillan, Toronto, 1975

MOVEMENT
A Novel in Stories

Valerie Miner

INTRODUCTION
by
SUSAN GRIFFIN

THE CROSSING PRESS / Trumansburg, New York 14886
The Crossing Press Feminist Series

*This book is dedicated to Carol Flotlin, who has been my
friend for twenty-five years, since we met on the playground
of Sacred Heart School in Bellevue, Washington.*

Copyright © 1982 Valerie Miner
The Crossing Press Feminist Series

Cover design by Mary A. Scott
Cover photograph by Marilyn Rivchin
Photograph of Valerie Miner by Betty Medsger
Book design by Martha J. Waters

Printed in the U.S.A.

Library of Congress Cataloging in Publication Data

Miner, Valerie.
    Movement, a novel.

    (The Crossing Press feminist series)
    I. Title. II. Series.
PS3563.I4647M6   813'.54   82-2543
ISBN 0-89594-079-5   AACR2
ISBN 0-89594-078-7 (pbk.)

ACKNOWLEDGMENTS

I thank all the Susans who conspired to make my life a better place: Susan Griffin in Berkeley, Susan Feldman in Toronto, Susan Faust in San Francisco, Suzan Donleavy in New York and Susan Addinell in London. Also inextricably part of this book were the women in my writing groups: Jana Harris, Kim Chernin, Mary Mackey, Eve Pell, Zoë Fairbairns, Michelene Wandor, Sara Maitland, Michele Roberts, Myrna Kostash, Charlene Spretnak. For their continuing faith and encouragement, I am grateful to Peggy Webb, Deborah Johnson, Carol Flotlin, Charlotte Sheedy, Leslie Gardner, Helen Longino and my mother, Mary Miner. Many thanks to Nancy K. Bereano who inspires but does not meddle in her good editing. We all owe to each other and to Jane and George and Virginia, the right to keep our writing on top of the blotter, in our own names, our sanity maintained, indeed, proclaimed, by our sisters.

A number of the stories first appeared in magazines or anthologies. "Novena," *Sinister Wisdom*; "Other Voices," *The Berkeley Monthly*; "Side/Stroke," *Womanblood* (Continuing Saga Press); "Sisterhood," *The Wild Iris*; "In The Company of Long Distance Peace Marchers," *Saturday Night*, Canada; "Maple Leaf or Beaver," *Prisma*; "The Right Hand on the Day of Judgment," *Spare Rib*, England. That story and "Afterlife" appear in *Tales I Tell My Mother* (South End Press, Boston). Three of the short-short stories were published together—"Aunt Victoria," "Cultured Green" and "Joan Crawford Revival"—in the *Boston Monthly* and *The Berkeley Monthly*.

Introduction

by
Susan Griffin

Movement is a book about change. In these pages Valerie Miner depicts movements within movements, public and private turns of heart, the permutations of consciousness in an innovative form which shifts from story to novel, and from past to present. The hero of this book, whose name is Susan, is a political activist and a writer. Her life is deeply enmeshed in the social events shared by a generation committed to ending injustice. She is part of the movement against the Vietnam War. Because she marries a draft resister, she moves with him to Canada. There she becomes part of a socialist movement, and gradually turns toward feminism.

Movement is also a book about consequence. Continually, Susan must live out, in her own body and soul, the implications of her political insights. And just as often, she is forced by experience to reconsider her commitments. Thus along with the same generation that questioned the causes of war and poverty, Susan moves past the traditional ways of living, and sharing lives. She looks for some center of meaning in sex and love, because along with freedom she seeks and finds a deepening knowledge of the world.

Each of the chapters of this book stands alone. Each can be read as a story, the way certain periods of one's life seem to have a definition and sense unto themselves. And inbetween these chapters, Valerie Miner has threaded a series of very short stories about others, strangers to Susan, not directly involved in any of the events of the narrative, peripheral. And yet, like the slight movements one captures at the edges of vision, these peripheral characters and their tales partake of the meanings which ring through Susan's life. For as much as this is a book about one fictional being, it is also a book about all our lives. We have all been touched by the social crises described here; we have all lived through the times which have inspired the questions Susan asks of life.

Like the work of Doris Lessing, or Marge Piercy, *Movement* preserves for us not only history, but more significant to the particular skill of a story teller, *sensibility*. The decades of the 1960's and 1970's were phenomenal not only for the happenings which journalists or newscasters might record, but also for the tone, the mood, the gestures, the configurations of people and remarks and styles, and above all a range of feeling. How often I have wished that someone tell these stories from our times. In one of the chapters Susan's editor, who is suffering the first symptoms of a nervous breakdown, deftly saves himself by taking credit for her work. That they both work for a radical magazine dedicated to equality and justice hardly affects his choices: she is not quite human to him. (It was this ironic juxtaposition of act and ideal that caused many women in this decade to sever themselves completely from men on the left.) In the character of Susan's husband we meet another archetype. The upper middle class young man who has the habit of calling his wife, whose mother is a waitress and father a seaman, "bourgeois." Predictably, his holier than thou radicalism fades with time. And Miner's reflection of our generation does not blur when she depicts women, either. She gives us a portrait of the young student, idealistic, eager, ignorant, full of vitality, love and naïveté. She presents us with the perpetually radical Wina wearing a "pink 'Frau Offensive' t-shirt. . .and declassé roach clip around her neck." And she captures the atmosphere through which these characters move, through which I myself remember moving. The politically correct, downwardly mobile pile of clutter left in a hallway. Exhaustion. Cold. Meetings. Personal rivalries described as philosophical differences. The ubiquitous Volkswagon Van. Cheap wine. Mattresses on the floor. The language of hope, despair, of charade.

Yet recognizable as these landscapes and the people in them are, they are not stereotypes bent on the wheel of polemic. Rather, the book draws a sharp and poignant outline around the dilemma we have all faced by confronting us always with the feeling of reality. No one here is idealized, not even the hero, and no one is villainized.

I was especially moved by a scene between Susan and a young Moroccan man as they discuss their life choices. Susan, instilled with a twentieth century North American sense of the self as sacred, cautions the young man not to live for others, not to be bound up in the expectations of his family. But of course. This is axiomatic for a character like Susan, even though she was born in the working class, as if her parents' very struggles were aimed to make her free of parental limitation. But when Susan tells the young man she does make choices for herself, he asks her, "Is this enough for you?" And she must agree that it is not. There is no resolution to this discussion between the two. They move on to another topic, and eventually into separate lives. Throughout the book, as in this scene, Miner does not leap to solve a question which is significant to our time for its irresolution.

And what a relief! The book is so witty. Spun throughout the extreme seriousness of a decade facing the devastations of the planet, the technological cruelties of modern warfare, the blistering conditions of racism, are movements of great humor in which sanity demands that those of us trying to take political responsibility for the future of the world laugh at ourselves.

What pompousness, what self-aggrandizement, what blustery romantic notions have characterized our struggles! When Susan muses about the Rock group, who pledged to lead a revolution, that they could not even hold their own band together, one feels along with the laughter, a heady breath of fresh air. Sometimes Miner's humor is gentle and tender, as in her description of a sixties costume party. And at other times, one feels this wit is close to the weeping of frustration, as for instance, when one character says of another, "She spoke English instead of rhetoric."

Miner's cameo portrait of the woman who spoke English and not rhetoric, is in a way a model for a commitment to social change toward which Miner's hero, Susan, moves. She is a "small grey-haired Montreal nurse who had worked in Vietnam during the Tet Offensive." (Between the lines I can almost hear the author say: she derived her rage from experience and not dogma.) "She delivered sense and feeling," Miner writes and, "She was more interested in peace than rubric and thus performed an intricate balance before this scrupulous congregation."

Throughout the rest of the book, Susan sorts out hollow rhetoric and performance from the daily passion of genuine caring. She asks the same questions of the Feminist movement that she asks of the anti-war and socialist movements. In a moment of tiredness, she asks, "Where was sisterhood now?" She had "given her loneliness to group consciousness, her anger to organized protest, her oppression to revolutionary retribution." But what does this mean? Even if she were free from oppression, what does this mean if there is no "afterlife"?

A heady, abstract, holier-than-life revolution can be, after all, only another excuse to avoid life. And yet, this is not a book to argue against movement. Rather it is from her deep passion for social justice which is the same as her passion for life that the hero, and the author, poses her questions. She turns back to her work with that tenaciousness of spirit that belongs only to the mature—for one must have been tried to possess it—and with the steadfast courage that belongs to those who, from years of small failures, know that we who are born of this troubled world, and would wish to end suffering, are not perfect, but we are beautiful.

Berkeley, California
Fall, 1981

◆

Postscript:

One last note. It is entirely fitting that The Crossing Press should publish this book. Its publishers possess the virtues of *Movement's* hero. This press has been with us for more than a decade (a long life for an alternative press) and shown all along a great courage and insight. They were very early publishers of feminist writing, before feminists became fashionable. (They were one of the first presses to publish any of my work.) Now, in these difficult times, when we have witnessed the closing down of, for instance, Diana Press, they have taken over the publication of several books we so need to have. And they continue to publish and distribute writing from those protest movements Susan might have belonged to: the antiwar movement, the prison rights movement, the movement for gay liberation. In these days when to work together seems so essential and yet so impossible, this press has quietly worked to print books from many different dissident movements and helped us all to understand perhaps, better, that in the end, we share a vision, and that none of our visions is complete without the insights of our sisters and brothers. I thank them for this.

Contents

Foreword

Movement is about a woman named Susan. It is a novel and a collection of short stories, exploring the territory between and beyond these forms. Most "chapters" follow a chronological sequence but also stand as stories on their own. I prefer such tales to longer narrative. The traditional novel has become an endurance test in which both the writer and the reader begin at the beginning and pursue the end without pause, in form, for reflection. Our lives are more flexible in time and space than most novels express. Life, or movement, is fantasy, memory, premonition, and the descriptions of this life should be layered.

Susan's stories are interwoven with short-short stories about completely different women who are experiencing other kinds of movement. I write these stories to break through the isolation and the individualism of the *Bildungsroman,* the conventional novel of development. Susan does not know, and may never meet, any of these women. Their stories are told as shadows and illuminations of our mutual momentum.

I
Movement

Susan slid the romaine leaf around the faded parquet bowl. It was too heavy with oil to curl through her fork. Larry Blake's special salad had more garlic than she remembered and the Coke tasted oversweet. Still, everything had a certain pungency compared to the stewed tea on which she had been surviving in London for years. A jock sat down in the opposite booth. Varsity most likely. He wore a pin-striped shirt under the Vaughn maroon sweater. Fraternities were popular again, she had heard, and everybody went to football games.

Susan felt personally offended, as if the last ten years hadn't happened. What did the 70's reap but an excuse for apathy? They hadn't "overcome" anything except their own idealism. Not completely true. But Berkeley seemed the same as before the Revolution—right down to these sunset scapes of San Francisco Bay on the restaurant walls. Her first year at Berkeley, she thought this was what you called an art exhibit. Some things *had* changed. She used to like Larry Blake's restaurant for the art exhibits.

Larry Blake's. What could you expect? Of course Guy would insist on meeting here, where they used to come for salads after studying. His conscience was a compass, always drawing them back around. Guy, her ex-husband, her first lover. None of the labels were either indelible or ephemeral enough. He was a ghost in her life; he would always be there, somewhere in the shadow of her former self. She looked at her watch and worried. It wasn't like Guy to be late.

Occasionally, Susan still wondered if she should have stayed with him. She might have been saner, safer in their academic coterie, drinking more gin and less tonic, serving cottage cheese and mandarin oranges on Centura unbreakable side plates. But the whole marriage stretched between "what-ifs" and "might-have-beens." And Susan was getting too old for abstractions.

She used to fantasize about what image she would bring back for him—successful critic, laid back vagabond, mad politico, artiste—and she used to worry about what he would choose to see. The six years since their divorce had spun as dizzily as a projector on rewind: *Liberation,* reel one. Now she wanted to tell him all she had learned about their marriage, him and herself. All that she had discovered about being a woman, about coming from an immigrant, unschooled, working class family. Although they had been married for seven years they had, like most proper Americans, ignored the delicate issues of class. She wanted to tell him about her failed contributions to the Mozambican revolution. About how she learned over and over that America was not the center of the world. And there was so much that was hard to speak in anecdotes. How she had moved from being a good Catholic girl to being a radical feminist. She wanted to tell him how she discovered she had a decent mind and then that she had deep feelings and fervent commitments and how she was just beginning to believe again that she had a soul. Even this morning she debated about wearing her Zanzibarian dress or her jeans and workshirt. Now, realizing how loud was the sameness around her, she understood that she didn't have to *project* any image. It didn't matter what he thought. It didn't matter if he showed up. And knowing this, she could wait a while longer.

Of course he would come back to the States when Carter pardoned the draft dodgers. Although it should have been amnesty rather than pardon, although deserters should have been included, although Guy and Susan had both sworn futures to Canada, the land of the possible, they would each come back. Guy had written to her: "Life is not a moral gymnasium." Susan had been able to appreciate Shaw only after the divorce. Yes, she had long known they would come back in different ways to different places in Berkeley.

The waiter deposited thick, bloody steaks in front of the jock and his girlfriend. Extra rare. She and Guy would have had just enough money now to order sirloin, to buy an el toro and paddle around the Bay. As it was, she could barely afford this salad. If nothing else, money marked the solid distinction between what might have been and what actually was.

Susan looked down at her notebook, pretending to read. The proposal for her next book. Had she brought it to save time or to show Guy or to hide behind at a solitary lunch?

They had been the ideal couple, much admired, often envied. Young, dedicated, vigorous. With a certain stylish earnestness. A handsome intelligence—they were the kind of couple who would be photographed for marijuana magazine ads in a few years. Political, unneurotic, talented, professional without being careerist. Comfortable in the funky apartment they shared with another couple above an Italian grocery in a West Indian district of Toronto. Even Guy's mother—after she had made her way through the neighbors—had to admit that the giant paisley cushions and the macrographics were "kind of cute and so resourceful." Guy was doing well in graduate school and Susan was making enough money from the magazine to buy a new sound system. Everything that might have been was happening.

So why was she unhappy? Her therapist told her she wasn't ready to grow up. Her Marx teacher told her she was tied to bourgeois gratifications. Her CR group told her she was confined by the patriarchal family. And everybody, despite their caveat, thought she and Guy had an open or healthy or growing relationship. Their friends were surprised when they split up: "Of all people." Susan was surprised that they were surprised.

She reached deep into her scarred leather purse and pulled out Guy's note. One o'clock. He said one o'clock. Now it was nearly 2:00 p.m.

In college, she would daydream about meeting her lover at an Italian restaurant with red-checked tablecloths and with Chianti bottles hanging from the ceiling. He would be a rather 50's Jack Lemmon lover. She never dreamed about her lover arriving, just about the waiting, about savoring his arrival. Now, she returned to her notebook, absently spooning the ice from her water glass to dilute the sweetness of the Coke. She used to do this with rum.

She remembered one stunning Bacardi afternoon during the last month of their marriage. She sat on the giant paisley cushion with page proofs strewn around her. *Appalachian Spring* was spinning on the Gerrard. She nibbled from a plate of carrots and raisins, sipping her third rum and Coke. For half an hour she had sat, staring blankly. There was something she had to figure out. Something about Guy's motivation for . . . now, what was it? Guy's motivation for . . . .

She had sat for another twenty minutes groping for the idea and releasing it just as it filed back into her head. Maybe she didn't want to settle the "marriage thing" after all. Maybe she had always known it would break down. No, the scary part was that there was nothing she had always known. This marriage was her fault, she realized, adding the rest of the rum to her Coke. When they were at Berkeley, she wanted to get married; he just wanted to live together. He said he needed a lot more backpacking, a lot more political work and, to be up front, a lot more screwing around before he settled into anything. But she won. They were married because, if nothing else, it was necessary for crossing borders.

The whole summer before the divorce had continued like that—phasing in and out, days sunk to the bottom of her glass. She switched to sherry, because it was cheaper, more convenient—for some reason. Everything was paced to possible depressions. Could she rationalize a drink for this? A little extra sleep for that? What the hell had happened to her? To them? It wasn't *his* fault. He was faithful. Now he was talking about kids and a communal house. Just what she had asked for. Why did she get herself into the labyrinth of drinking and sleeping that desultory summer?

Guy's note, she read it again. Yes, one o'clock. This was his first communication in three years, despite a dozen letters from her. He used to be the prolific one. He had maintained the correspondence with their families. He was the sentimental one. And now?

Often in those last days he had tried to relieve her spells of depression. On their seventh anniversary he suggested a good dinner at Damarco's. They both tried to enjoy the vignette. Red-checked tablecloths. Chianti bottles. (But she had no one to wait for. They had come together.) Guy ordered them the second most expensive thing on the menu. They talked about plans for the summer and about a friend from Berkeley who would visit the next week. He said he wanted to tell her something and he hoped it wouldn't sound too soppy. He rather liked being married to a frizzy radical. Of course he wasn't politically impotent just because he was an intellectual. His work in the dialectical influences on Freud was important for the Movement too. He wasn't going to apologize. Anyway, he knew *she* wasn't judgmental; that was one of the reasons he would always love her.

After that meal at Damarco's, she really craved a liqueur. Kahlua or Tia Maria. No, she had promised herself—only three drinks a night. What the hell was wrong with her anyway? Why was she constricted by his good will? Guilty. Yes, she had used this marriage for her own ends, for support and confidence. Now she needed to stand alone. Maybe not completely guilty. "A mortal sin is a knowing offense against . . . ." She sipped her coffee slowly, trying not to conjure the soothing qualities of Kahlua. The change had come naturally, at least imperceptibly. They had both changed. They weren't the same people. God, it all sounded so trite, so hollow, so boring. No, this couldn't—wouldn't—happen to them, she told herself. They would talk when they got to bed. This air was too close with smoke and parmesan for sense. Once they got out of this place, they would be all right.

Neither of them felt like going to bed. Guy suggested Scrabble. She agreed. Her first word was "cache."

"That's a double word score," he smiled, "twenty-four points."

From that moment, that move, Susan never again doubted that they would separate. And understanding so, she didn't have much left to figure out.

She did wonder, now as she waited at Larry Blake's, whether Guy still played Scrabble.

Joan Crawford Revival

He didn't usually pick up hitchhikers. But she was wearing this green Joan Crawford hat. He hadn't seen those broad-rimmed hats since his kid sister used to mug around in them. Green felt with a red polka dot sash. Ah, what the hell, he was an hour up on his time. He'd make it by tomorrow, easy, even if he had to go out of his way to drop her off. He supposed that's what you did with hitchhikers. Anyway, he was fed up with these radio phone-ins. Wouldn't mind a little company. So he eased over to the curb. She looked up, delighted.

"Where ya heading?" he shouted into the frozen morning.

"East," she said briskly, "as far as you're going East."

"Well, I can't take you to the Atlantic Ocean. But I am going as far as Salt Lake City. Hop in if you like." He thought maybe he sounded a little too flip.

She grinned, piled her satchels in the back seat and slid into the front. She fastened the seat belt with the same dispatch as his wife and he noticed how different the two of them were. Different spirit. From the road, he had guessed that she was mid-twenties, like his sister. But now he could see she was at least thirty-five. Interesting how some women just stay young.

He felt her looking at him looking at her. He couldn't just ask why she was going East. He didn't want to start off with something boring like that. "Running away from home?" he chuckled.

"Yes," she said, unpinning her hat, placing it on her lap and watching the road ahead.

II

Maple Leaf or Beaver

"Will you check the turnoff for Highway 80?" The first thing Guy had said for three hours.

"Just past Reno," Susan said. "And from there, let's see, it's about 2,000 miles."

He smiled and turned on the radio.

By the Time I Get to Phoenix.

Susan watched the dark, bearded man behind the wheel of this van which carried all her belongings—grapefruit crates of clothes and books and the hope of silver-coated wedding presents. The van, itself, was a wedding gift, purchased with a rather grand check from Guy's father four years ago. She thought the van suited them perfectly: sensible and unpretentious. She hated cushy sedans reeking of new naugahyde and isolated from the world by shock absorbers.

"Doesn't this remind you of a covered wagon?" Susan asked, nervously twisting a curl of her long brown hair.

"Not exactly," Guy said. "I mean, we are wearing seat belts."

"How far do you think we'll get today?" she asked. She didn't say, "What if we can't get across the border?"

"I dunno," he said. "Let's just drive 'till we're tired." He turned up the radio.

By the Time I Get to Phoenix . . . .

She didn't really want to talk now, either. She would have a whole life to talk with this taciturn man who was her husband. Whoever he was. Whomever he would become. "Jesus Christ." Her mother had suggested the resemblance soon after she found out Guy was going to be a professor. The image changed to "Rasputin" when mother saw Guy on KPIX, burning his draft card. Susan, herself, had always thought Guy looked like Peter Yarrow on the cover of *Album 1700*. How could she have known that *The Great Mandella* would let them off at a strange border?

◇

She wanted to be with Guy. She loved Guy's commitment and intelligence. She enjoyed being part of his family. They argued about theatre and read *The Economist*. They were interested in her work. They asked about propaganda and objectivity and literary journalism. Not that her own mother wasn't interested. She had always wanted Susan to be happy. She waited on tables in dingy restaurants for twenty years so her daughter could be happy in America. Susan appreciated that her family were good, hard-working people. But they never understood her wanting to go to college, never asked questions about her writing. Maybe she was a little ashamed of their grammar and their bowling trophies. Yes, she was ashamed of being ashamed. And eventually her mother approved of Guy Thompson, approved of her marrying up, although she didn't want her moving away. Certainly not moving as far as Canada. Somehow all of Susan's shame and guilt and regret about their separation got lost in those arguments about Vietnam, Laos and Cambodia. But there had been no choice, no choice about the war.

◇

Susan wanted to stop the van and ask, "What if we don't get in?" Instead, she kept her silence and watched the asphalt hem into brown Nevada hills. The border guards weren't allowed to inquire about the draft; all the selective service counselors had said so. Still, gossip was that some guys got turned away. What if they couldn't get in at Windsor? Should they try Sarnia? Would they hide out in the north Michigan woods? Susan and Guy had carefully discussed the leaving. They were reconciled about not being able to return to the States. But what if they had nowhere to go? She refused to think about it.

◊

She thought, instead, about last night's conversation with Mother.

"It's against the law," her mother said.

"Mother, we've been through this before."

"You're breaking the law, both of you."

"Is it a good law? Is it a good war?"

"Why can't you get out of it legally, like your brother Bill?"

"You know that we've tried, for eighteen months, to get out of it. As for Bill—Bill does ballistics research. That's the same as fighting."

"Better that Guy go to jail, like Joan Baez' husband."

"Mother, you're not honestly suggesting that."

"And what about your job? You're going to leave all that, chasing off to Canada with some man?"

"Well, this is interesting. Since when have you found my career more sacred? Besides, it was a mutual decision. We're both resisting."

Silence. Patience, Susan reminded herself. It was important that this conversation end well.

"Mother?"

"Yes?"

"When you left Scotland to come to the States, it was your choice."

"That was entirely different. It was money. I left so I could make a living somewhere. But you, you've got a college education. You could have a nice home here. Listen," she spoke more slowly and softly now, "every country has its problems."

"Mom, phone calls from Canada are going to be expensive. Why don't we make the best of this?"

"Of course dear, you're right, dear. Remember I love you. Remember . . . ."

Susan stared out the van window at the endless road ahead. And she thought about how Guy's parents were such a contrast as they sat around the family breakfast table this morning.

Guy and Susan had risen wordlessly and slipped on the matching brown and beige terry cloth robes his parents had given them.

Dr. Thompson was sitting at the oak table, slowly rotating a crystal glass of orange juice. Mrs. Thompson called from the kitchen, "Perhaps you should go and wake them, darling?"

"No, no need," laughed Guy. "We wouldn't want to be late for . . . ."

His father looked up expectantly, like a schoolmaster waiting for the wrong answer.

"For, for the future," stumbled Guy.

"Precisely," said Dr. Thompson.

Mrs. Thompson nodded briskly to her husband and smiled to her children, "Sleep well, sweet ones?"

"Just fine, thank you," Susan sang and followed her into the kitchen while Guy took the seat next to his father.

The coffee had started to perk. Eggs lay out on the stainless steel counter. Room temperature by now. Ready to be boiled. White against coldwater steel. Susan had never cooked in Mrs. Thompson's kitchen. She had never done anything except wash the dishes. She didn't even dry them because she couldn't tell where all the fancy plates belonged. Susan picked up the eggs one by one with a slotted spoon, submerging them in the hot waves. From the oven, bearclaw pastries sweated sweetly. Mrs. Thompson had been saving them in the fridge since Tuesday. Just as Susan reckoned the eggs were ready, Mrs. Thompson reached in front of her, switched off the gas and placed them in four china egg cups at the end of a silver tray. Susan carried them into the dining room with acolytic care.

Usually the oak breakfast table was spread with green pages from the *Chronicle*. This morning, it was bare, save for two crystal glasses of orange juice slowly rotating in their water-marks and the $50 bill which lay between them.

"Be sensible for once, Guy. Your mother and I just want to feel that you're eating properly on your trip north."

("He always makes it sound like a polar bear expedition," Guy would say.)

"Thanks, Dad, but we're both old enough to take care of each other." Last night they had worried together about making it to the end of the month. Guy looked at Susan nervously.

Dr. Thompson flushed. He always bore anger with florid Victorian dignity. "If you can't accept a little help at a time like this, I don't know what's happened to the concept of family."

Susan picked up the $50 and put it on the tray. "It's very kind of you," she said and bent down to kiss her father-in-law.

"That's a girl," said Dr. Thompson.

Such a polite, distracted breakfast, the kind of meal you have with fellow travellers—everyone caught up in their own thoughts, random references to mileage and time of arrival. No mention of departure. After an hour there was no more silence left. Since they had packed the van the previous evening, they only had to load their suitcases now.

And so it ended quietly, without any of the strain or re-crimination or tears of the last twelve months. They drove down Fenwick and past the yellow adobe house with the sleek Irish setter. She reflected numbly that Guy's mother hadn't cried. A tear escaped down his nose, dripping from his moustache like sweat. He asked her to check that they had all the maps.

◇

It was a 2,500 mile waiting room. She read him *Newsweek* and *Ramparts* and *The Making of a Counterculture* as they rode the rainy highways between hashbrowns and scrambled eggs and double cheeseburgers.

By the Time I Get to Phoenix was top of the charts in every small-town radio station.

12

NBC Monitor analyzed President Nixon. (*President* Nixon. That still seemed unreal to her.)

CBS repeated instant news. Instant news.

For miles before and after Salt Lake City they heard engagements, marriages, items for barter, prayers of the day.

By the Time I Get to Phoenix . . . .

They were cutting right across the country without being there. Rain, asphalt, gas station Coke machines, vacant winter-rate motels, rain, asphalt.

"Shall I read the business section?" she asked.

"I dunno," he said. "What's it about?"

Silence.

"Guy?"

"Yeah, hon?"

"What are you thinking about, dear?"

"An article on spider monkeys in the *Journal of Primatologists*, February issue."

"Swell."

"What?"

"Isn't that fucker ever going to get to Phoenix?"

"What?"

"Damn radio," she switched it off. "Inane."

He nodded absently and turned on Instant News, adding, "Maybe in Canada the songs will be in French and we won't be able to understand them."

She didn't say, "What if we don't get in."

◊

Last summer there had been no barriers. On their pup tent trip around North America, they had looped back and forth from Plattsburg to Montreal to Rochester to Toronto to Detroit to Calgary to Seattle. A trial journey. If they could survive in a pup tent, they could survive exile. At that time, Canada was one romantic option. They were still negotiating with the draft board, medical school, Oxford, the Navy Reserve. Canada seemed like the land of the possible. Everything was possible until December when only the Navy Reserve and Canada were left. They chose Canada. She knew they were right, of course. Of course, as long as they got in.

◇

So this year they celebrated his birthday at the Sleepy Hollow Motel in Iowa City. They didn't feel like dining out. She sneaked the Coleman stove into their room and reheated pea soup. They ate silently, stretched out on the coral chenille bedspread, watching *Marcus Welby, M.D.*

"I'm going to miss Robert Young," she sighed.

"What kind of shit is that?" he said. "Talk about reactionary values."

"Oh, I don't know. Remember *Father Knows Best?* Kathy, Bud, Betty. There was always a sense of fairness."

He grimaced, as he often did, enjoying her optimism, but baffled about how it could be so thoroughly misplaced.

"The Andersons," she continued. "The kind of nice, stable family everybody wants. And remember Franco, the Italian gardener?"

"Yeah, I remember. A thoroughly racist role."

"My, weren't you perceptive at ten years old?"

"Silly to argue," he said. "Anyway, you'll be able to watch Robert Young in Canada. They get all the Buffalo stations."

"Cultural imperialism," she agreed sardonically. But this reassured her. And she was glad Guy didn't want to make love but just to hang on. She would feel better the next day when they saw Hank and Sara in Ann Arbor.

It would be good to have friends living that close to Canada. They could all go camping in northern Ontario together. So much clean, green space. Sometimes she thought of Canada as a huge National Park. Maybe they could all meet for weekends in Montreal. Not that she wanted to huddle with Americans. She had heard of these "Amex communities," full of heavy "political people." She always felt nervous around political people. Not tough enough. They were so suspicious that they made her feel like she really was a CIA agent. She was a war protestor, not a radical. Even her own family agreed after the Cambodian invasion (well, for them, it had been after Kent State) that the War was wretched. To her, Canada was the only reasonable choice. And now, having made that choice, she and Guy were traitors, idealists or good political people depending on who was lecturing or interviewing them.

"Do you feel political?" she asked the next morning in Illinois.

"I feel tired," he answered. "Why don't you read the book review section?"

◇

Hank and Sara's apartment might have been astral-projected from Berkeley—with the same peeling rattan chairs, the same odor of cat pee in the yellow rug. After their famous chile and some good Colombian dope, they were all back on Euclid Avenue.

"Medical school is a drag so far," said Hank. "Two of my ancient professors look like founding members of the AMA."

"You don't have to say that for me," returned Guy. "I'm glad you got a draft deferment. And I'm just as glad I didn't get into med school. Come on, now, it's cool, isn't it?"

"Aw, I don't know. But I have met some good people in the Vietnam Aid Committee."

"Some good political people?" asked Susan.

He nodded solemnly and pulled out a white booklet. "Here it is, *Manual For Draft Age Immigrants To Canada.* Everyone is using it. I mean it's been good for some people passing through."

Susan was touched, and very frightened. This was like a refugee visa. It reminded her of the job permit which Mother kept under the gloves in the top bureau drawer. Thin blue paper and black ink, "culinary worker." She remembered Rosa Kaburi, her fourth grade friend from Hungary, who had told her about the name tags on their wrists and how they were inspected for lice by the immigration officer. But this was Canada, she reminded herself. You didn't even need a passport to enter.

15

Sara sat forward. "Actually, we've been talking a lot about our connection in all of this. I mean, of course the phone is tapped. But you should feel there's a way to contact us if you need help. Maybe a code word. Maybe 'maple leaf' or 'beaver.'"

"Or 'help,'" laughed Susan. "We'll be the safe ones."

They spent the evening counting up immigration credits— Susan spoke French and had relatives in Canada; he had more years in university.

"Kind of classist, isn't it?" asked Guy.

"Every country has its problems," said Hank.

"I have five more points than you," said Susan.

"Doesn't count," said Sara. "A wife goes through on her husband's points."

Irritated, Susan thought about this new women's lib business, and resolved to do some reading. She wondered, dopily, what Guy would do if she became a raving feminist.

Hank picked up the booklet and ripped off the cover. "Don't let them see it when they search you at the border. Stick it inside one of your chemistry texts or somewhere."

The dope wore off quickly. Guy shaved his beard. Disguises were prepared in rote timelessness. Susan ironed her shirtwaist dress and set her hair. Once these chores were done, the evening lost shape. They crawled into the sleeping bags and read Hank's and Sara's new *Newsweek* before falling asleep.

The next morning, Susan jiggled out of the sleeping bag and walked over to the picture window. Grey. The fog outside the third floor window overlooking Pauline Street was as colorless as the apartment walls. Susan reheated the coffee and found some more bearclaw pastries. Were bearclaws Californian? Was she more Californian or American? Could she be a Canadian? Canada was just over the bridge. Just across the border. Only a few miles away. Canada, land of the free. No reason to believe in Canada. ("What an idealist," her brother Bill had said. "What are the choices?" Susan had said.) So now it was to be Canada. A country big enough to believe in.

Yes, she did believe they would be admitted.

"Breakfast, sir?" she said, setting a tray on the floor, next to where he lay, still cosy under the down.

"Feels more like Extreme Unction," he said.

"Good code word."

They laughed, as easily as if they were back in Berkeley.

◇

Detroit was the classic exit. She recalled headlines from the '66 riots. She remembered that unmailed thank you note to Aunt Martha and Uncle Cardiologist who sent them an American flag for their wedding from Grosse Pointe. (Mother insisted it wasn't a joke.) The ride up Michigan Avenue was horrific. Every white man looked like he was about to duck into a telephone booth and emerge in a Klan hood. The blacks frightened her like no one in Oakland had scared her for years. Her racism? Their hostility? They drove past Bertram's department store where Aunt Martha had bought that pinafore when Susan was eight. (Susan's mother had inhaled sharply when she saw the pink and grey box. Bertram's was a *very* fine store. Aunt Martha always sent things from very fine stores. Mother might have sent more pink and grey boxes herself if she hadn't married a feckless sailor and moved to California.) Grey, humid Detroit heat. Petulant showers and then sudden sun evaporating everything. What if they didn't get in? Just get out of Detroit. Love it or leave it. Just get out.

◇

"Shit, Susan, this is the tunnel. I told you we wanted the bridge. Everyone says the bridge is an easier crossing."

"No, they say it's quicker, but the guards at the tunnel are easier."

"Hell, Susan, don't you remember what Hank said about the deserter from Georgia? Shit, Susan."

Her voice was blocked with tears.

"Just tell me the way to the bridge," he barked. "I'm the one who's driving the van. I'm the one who's resisting the damn draft."

17

"Oh, I see," she turned to him, glared at him, raising her voice. "And I suppose I'm just along for the ride?"

He rubbed the back of his hand along her cheek and kept his eyes on the traffic ahead. "I'm sorry, hon. It's our decision. Let's not get *at* each other. It'll be over in an hour. We'll be in Canada. Maple leaf or beaver," he tried to laugh. Then he lowered his voice to soothing. "We'll be OK in Canada."

She didn't say, "if we get in." She said, "It looks as if the Ambassador Bridge is just about ten blocks from here."

◇

When they passed the U.S. border guards, she wanted to wave or give them the finger, but their escape was too tenuous. A small sign in the middle of the bridge said, "Welcome to Canada. Bienvenue au Canada." Before she noticed it, they had pulled up to the Canadian border guard.

"Good afternoon," he said. "What is the purpose of your visit?"

Guy's face grew pale. She looked for reassurance in his familiar features and all she could see was his pale.

"My wife and I would like to apply for landed immigrancy."

("My wife and I," she thought. They had married for this charade. "Immigrancy." Ellis Island. Her mother and Rosa Kaburi. New World. But no one would muck up their name here. Not a High Anglo name like Thompson. She knew what she was doing when she took that name.)

"Eh, what was that? Could you speak up, please?"

Those were the right words. She knew they were the right words. What kind of game was this fellow running?

"OK" the guard said finally. "Go to the green building over there after you've filled out these forms."

"Out," Canadian "out." He hadn't smiled.

"My wife and I would like to immigrate to Canada."

"Did you bring your gear with you?" Another foreign official. Never before had she thought of Canadians as so foreign.

18

"Gear?" Guy asked.

"Furniture," barked the official, "pots, pans, baby carriage."

"Oh, my parents are sending up that stuff," said Guy, who was always good at charades. "We do have a few things in the car."

Susan wondered what they would think when they saw the sleeping bags, typewriters, guitars. Hippies? Actually, it was true that Guy's mother insisted on sending up the mahogany bedroom set once they got settled.

"Draft dodger?" the guard asked casually.

"In fact," Guy answered coolly, "I'm a teaching assistant in primatology at the University of Toronto."

"I'm the draft dodger," she joked, feeling vomit rise in her throat with the forced laughter.

The guard smiled and nodded to the door with a grey mesh window.

"Don't have nothing to do with me anyway. *He'*ll see you in a minute." He returned to their forms to make sure they had left no white spaces.

"What about the *Manual*?" she whispered.

Guy looked confused. Or was it annoyed? Maybe he was signaling her to shut up. But the question was important in case the van were searched. She leaned over and whispered, "Did you put it in the chemistry book?"

"You were the one who had it last," he said between his teeth and then turned back to a travel brochure. "Did you know that Nova Scotia is the only region outside Scotland to have a registered tartan?"

Her stomach turned. She rummaged for a Tums in her purse. There, bunched with the birth certificates and marriage license, was the *Manual*. Did they search purses?

"Mr. and Mrs. Thompson?"

They followed another guard into a small, spare room. Guy didn't have to repeat so much this time. Maybe the acoustics were better. Maybe he was learning Canadian. The officer asked them questions which they had already answered on the application.

"And you, Mrs. Thompson, what do you do?"

She paused for a moment, as if listening for her mother-in-law (Will the *real* Mrs. Thompson please speak up?) and then she answered, "I'm a teacher." The words came too easily. She dreaded hearing them. It had taken her a year to feel able to say "writer," when people inquired. "Teacher" was just what she wasn't going to be her whole life. However, they needed teachers in Canada, in places like Baffin Island. She would do anything to get them in.

He checked their diplomas, licenses and bank books. Pedigrees seemed to be in order. That was all for now. No questions about why they wanted to immigrate. No speeches about the Great National Park or the three party system or the ethnic mosaic. He had *no* more questions.

"If you'll wait here, I'll be right back with an answer for you."

When he closed the door, she looked at Guy for the first time since they entered the room.

"Your purse," he said.

Her purse lay open on her lap to the *Manual For Draft Age Immigrants To Canada.*

He squeezed her hand. "Don't worry," he said.

She didn't have the strength to squeeze back. She just wanted to throw up. Of course good immigrants don't throw up. The guard might think she had typhoid or something. She stared at the grey mesh window.

"That's it, Mr. and Mrs. Thompson."

The immigration officer was handing something to Guy.

"That's it," Guy said, louder, to her.

The man had his hand on Guy's shoulder, "Bloody awful war."

◇

Toronto. Two hundred miles. The road signs had crowns on them. "Welcome to Canada. Bienvenue au Canada."

She turned on CBC to distract them from Windsor.

"War Measures Act . . . . "

The city seemed to mirror Detroit through foul Lake Michigan. And the water looked just as dead from this side.

". . . War Measures Act. Prime Minister Trudeau said in a press conference in Ottawa this afternoon that the decree of martial law will be in effect all over the country. Primary surveillance will take place in Quebec. In Montreal so far, thirteen people suspected of knowing about the Pierre La Porte kidnapping have been taken to jail. The CBC has received no official communiques from the FLQ. Martial law is . . . . "

"Find some music, will you?" said Guy.

"In French?" she asked.

The Common Stinkweed

Her father offered a Harris tweed suit and a silk blouse if she would go out and get a real job. "Why, that would cost a hundred quid," she exclaimed. Her father nodded, threateningly, generously—she couldn't distinguish anymore. They each laughed it off rather too loudly. He complained that she always knew more about what she didn't want than what she did want.

Not true. She knew she wanted to go to America. It would be different when she got to America. She didn't know what started this "Yankophilia" as she called it. Maybe it began in University when she met all those kids from L.A. She liked the offhand way they referred to "school" rather than university, the way they called professors by their first names and the way they called lecturers "professors." They had turned her on to grass (much more sensible than lager, not as fattening and no hangover) and to their music. Funky rock. There was something so down-to-earth (now, that had to be an American term) and honest about their music. It wasn't like that cerebral Pink Floyd nonsense. She loved denim. So unpretentious, like everything American.

Originally, she had planned to leave in September. But Diane's husband left her. The poor girl was at the end of her tether. So she gave Diane a few quid and a little time. Diane would need company for a couple of months at least.

She looked forward to airletters from her friends in West Virginia ("Did you catch *Deliverance?* Have you heard the music, seen the quilts?"); and friends in Washington D.C. (Fred was a Nader's Raider in the nerve center of American corruption); and her old beau in Bellingham (Those photos of mountain goats in the Olympic range were tacked around the ancient victrola in her bedsit).

She painted on weekends and was rather proud of a couple of watercolors that she gave her parents for Easter. However, she knew she wouldn't really get into her art until America. So much to paint there. Mary told her they would take a caravan—no, it was called a trailer—through the Grand Canyon and up the California coast to visit Len. Then she would find the Black Hills of South Dakota and the Dells in Wisconsin and the Fall in New England and the green fields of Mississippi. She consumed travel books, started reading regional fiction and fell in love with William Faulkner.

Meanwhile, another six months passed as she worked in the Engineering Library, cataloguing journal articles. A tedious job, yes Mother, beneath her talents. But it allowed time to think, to plan. Somehow she had made herself indispensable. It was a curious circle: the harder she worked to make money for the trip, the more difficult it was to get away for things like a visa and tickets.

She almost made the plane reservation the morning she heard that radio program about the common stinkweed. The Common Stinkweed. Bloody English even made class distinctions about plants. As if people had the leisure to be botanized at eight in the morning. The BBC's mentality was absolutely stifling.

The news wasn't any better. So lethargic. So sober. Almost as if the broadcasts were conjured to reassure. She could never understand her parents' commitment to Britain, their unflagging patriotism and their maudlin memories about "finest hours." As far as she could tell, even the War had been distilled and produced by the BBC.

Well, she couldn't really leave before Christmas, could she? Mother would be too disappointed. It was bad enough to be going away for a year. Actually, it might be longer, but she wasn't going to upset them until she knew definitely. She decided she shouldn't go before January. That was a proper time for a fresh start. Then it would all be different, in America.

III

In the Company of Long-Distance Peace Marchers

They said it would be the last peace march. Peace was at hand. The treaty would be signed that week. Susan marched because she believed—in her most optimistic soul— that it *was* the last peace march. She marched because she believed—in her most realistic head—that there would never be a last peace march. She didn't know why she went.

She didn't want to go. She wanted to stay at home and do all the editing and writing and reading that had fulfilled her life for the last year. But she couldn't stay home. Maybe she went out of faith in ceremony, in public proclamation of principle. Since girlhood, she had been possessed by processions and professions of faith. In fact, when she didn't go to Mass the next morning one of the small excuses (she still needed excuses, but only small ones now) was having attended the march.

How many antiwar demonstrations had she joined here in Toronto or back in San Francisco? Not enough, evidently. Marches were as much part of her immigrant identity in Canada as "festas" were for Italo-Canadians. Cultural critics classified demonstrations as "60's phenomena," but the decade was two years past and she was still marching. Once she expected marches and chants and speeches to change things. Yes, she expected the Moratorium in November, 1969, to bring change. Thousands of people marching across San Francisco to Golden Gate Park. They were going to start a revolution according to Crosby, Stills, Nash and Young. (Hell, *they* couldn't stay together long enough to run a rock group.) Yes, she did believe it then. And in the sense that she didn't want to be a liberal cop-out, she still believed it. A little.

Usually Susan went to marches with Guy. But he was working on his thesis today. "My research is political," he had said that morning even though she hadn't asked him why he wasn't going and, in fact, was glad to be going alone. "There are other ways to be a political person," he protested. She nodded, thinking how she was almost comfortable calling herself a "political person" after two years in Canada.

So after all this you would think she might know something about marches. That they never start on time, for instance, like poetry readings and other secular rituals. However, when she realized she was going to be "late," she flew out the front door, worried the subway down to her stop and then raced to the Metropolitan United Church. Inside, four hundred people sat listening to speeches. A warm up. An examination of conscience. It would last for another forty-five minutes.

Rhetoric. Did these phrases ever mean anything? "Fighting imperialism in the people's struggle," or was it "Life, liberty and the pursuit of happiness"? Rhetoric was a bond, a common language. They knew the platitudes by rote—the middle-aged minister who spoke first and the young Trotskyite who spoke last. Peace and self-determination. Amen. Right on. Folded hands. Clenched fists.

But the woman who spoke in the middle, the small, grey-haired Montreal nurse who had worked in Vietnam during the Tet Offensive, offered more than rhetoric. She gave figures about Canadian complicity in the war. She tied the Indochinese fighting to other struggles. "I don't know if I'm the first woman to speak from this pulpit, but I know that I won't be the last." She delivered sense and feeling. She was more interested in peace than rubric and thus performed an intricate balance before this scrupulous congregation.

The people didn't look much different from those Susan marched with in California. Mostly young and blue-jeaned. Their hair was longer than two years ago; their clothes were heavier than those worn in San Francisco. Otherwise, they were the same people. The poor students and lefties wore balled sweaters and rotting shoes. The week-end working class insulated themselves in $60 army green parkas. The marshals, veterans of other marches, wore red arm bands. The photographers—there were going to be lots of pictures for the time capsule—posed Nikons and Pentaxes at the speakers and listeners. The skinny man from CKEY radio had pinned a large red PRESS sign to his cashmere lapel. Freaks in peacoats and linty mufflers passed the silver collection plates for publicity funds as the speakers harangued from a stained glass sanctuary.

Out in the vestibule, portable bookstores were assembled. The Vanguard man peddled inspirations from Marx, Ché, Engels, Trotsky. Friends greeted each other after long holiday absences. She recognized several feminists, a *Guerilla* reporter, the lawyer for a political refugee, a friend of a friend who wrote Young Socialist articles, a Cabbagetown teacher, the editor of an American exile magazine and several still nameless people she always saw at demonstrations.

Susan thought how her mother would cringe at all this "Communism," would worry for her daughter. Mother had finally become reconciled that she and Guy were draft dodgers. She had stopped calling them "deserters." She just wanted them to come home.

Ranks formed outside the church. The January winds were a cold shock. She wanted to walk with the women's contingent, so she headed for the banner reading, "In Solidarity with Our Vietnamese Sisters."

"Did you hear the woman's speech?" grinned Hilary. "She got the biggest applause."

"Yeah, it was the best one," said Elizabeth. "She spoke

English instead of rhetoric. She actually brought up some facts."

They talked about the sameness. Not just the same people, but the same worn signs, "End Canadian Complicity." The same destination, the U.S. Consulate. The same chants, "Stop the bombing; stop the war." But the litany changed somewhat today, abridging the latest headlines, "One point peace plan; no Canadian troops." And when three men started, "Ho, Ho, Ho Chi Minh . . . ," the women interrupted with, "Madame, Madame, Madame Binh, Madame Binh is going to win."

Lesbians, Susan noticed, a lot of these feminists were lesbians. She felt the same around lesbians as she used to feel around political people. "Not tough enough." A little scared. Did you have to be a lesbian to be a feminist? Could they tell she wasn't a lesbian?

They all crashed the Saturday afternoon shopping scene with their chants and leaflets and posters. More of the shoppers were with them than against them. Most of these good citizens just wanted to walk from Eaton's department store to Simpson's department store without a hassle. One aging wino, who had been following since the Fred Victor Mission, picked up a placard, "End U.S. Aggression," and joined the march. By the time they reached Queen and Yonge Streets, the contingents had lost all definition. The women's group was jostled into the Evangelicals for Social Action, the NDP and the Harbord Collegiate Student Council. Susan recognized one woman and asked her where the rest of the feminist crew had gone. She shrugged her shoulders, "Who knows? It's always like this."

"Oh, you have an American accent," Susan said, trying to start a conversation.

"Yes, I'm afraid so. It's not a very pleasant thing to be an American." Emily was a social worker. Her shiny white hair was pulled back into a pony tail. She had brought her teenage kids north last year. Not the stereotyped expatriate, Susan thought.

"Canada gives us much more of a chance at life," Emily was saying. "You just can't live in the States any more. I've tried to change things. I remember marching in a Korean War protest twenty years ago . . . . "

"But don't you ever regret coming?" asked Susan. "Don't you miss your friends, your relatives back there?"

"Yes, but I don't regret coming. Not one bit."

Susan wanted to tell her that she, too, was an American. That she, too, was glad she left the States. But that she did have some regrets. Before this voice would surface, the crowd surged ahead of them, onto the street.

"Good," shouted Emily huskily, "We're taking the streets."

She and Susan moved off the sidewalk, remaining close to the curb, wending their way through the stalled traffic on Yonge Street. People in the cars looked startled at first. Some of them began to wave.

"This must be like a three-D drive-in movie for them," said Susan, smiling at the amused faces behind the windshields.

"See how they're smiling," said Emily. "If this happened in the States, they'd be scowling and cursing. See, there's a difference in the countries for you, right there."

They didn't have the streets for long before policemen and their horses ushered everyone back on the sidewalk. Susan noticed no tear gas or helicopters or bayonets. No real confrontation. However, the marchers did keep careful watch on the horses' hooves.

Some of the feminists were talking about the aggressiveness of Americans in Canada. Susan observed that many radical Americans were just as jingoistic as Republican businessmen.

"You're absolutely right," said one arm of the Women's Place banner. "A lot of lefties think they know everything because they've struggled in America. They try to take over the Canadian Movement. I know, I'm an American, myself."

Susan didn't divulge her nationality, wanting to leave the illusion that there were at least some Canadians in the procession.

As they walked by the cluster of stereo and camera shops

near Dundas Street, a young man shouted at them, "So what do Canadians have to do with the bloody war?"

Emily instructed him that over 400 Canadian companies made parts for the U.S. Defense Department.

"Well, you gotta have a job, somehow."

As he argued, his Newfoundland accent thickened. Susan saw that he was missing five front teeth.

"Sure," Susan shouted, "but there are better ways to make money." Later, all she could remember about him was his missing teeth.

"Stop the bombing; stop the war. Stop the bombing; stop the war." A sound truck proceeded them, an electronic cheerleader. "Stop the bombing; stop the war."

Susan felt an odd loneliness in all this community spirit. Once she lost her friends in the crowd, she had walked for blocks in silent solidarity. Slightly disconnected. Maybe that's why she had started talking with Emily. But after a while, after they had exchanged enough impressions about the war and expatriation and Canadians and Americans, Susan needed to move away from the echo. She began to listen to the other conversations around her.

An old man in a dark suit was arguing with a scraggly graduate student.

"Don't you think you're a little presumptuous, telling the North Vietnamese how to negotiate—all this one point peace plan stuff?"

"But listen, a negotiated settlement with peace keeping forces is just a stall for Thieu. The only way for the country to be run by its citizens is for the U.S. to get the hell out of there."

In front of Susan, a two-year old cried in her mother's arms.

"Why don't you take her for a while, Steve?"

He exchanged his placard for his kid. "OK Sugar, you wanta come to Daddy?"

A small boy carried a homemade sign, "Victory to the Vietnamese Revolution." His mother held her mink hat down against the winds.

Two freaks were filming the march from a car near Queen's Park. "It looks great," one of them shouted. "The march must be a mile long."

Emily had found another companion. "You know, I did this stupid thing. I wore tennis shoes and my feet are absolutely freezing. You'd think I'd know better after all these years. I've been marching since the Korean War."

A small, red-faced man was talking about Belfast bombings with a young woman. As Susan moved closer to listen, the women stared at her suspiciously. She warned the man to lower his voice, mumbling something about CIA agents. So much for solidarity.

The procession was approaching the American Consulate. Their litany grew louder. "One point peace plan; U.S. out now." The signs rocked above their heads. "End Canadian Complicity." "Stop Phallic Imperialism."

The big, white Consulate building was guarded by fifteen pallid policemen. Four cops in a row with regulation small moustaches. Susan thought of her brother Bill's toy soldiers in their slim, dashing patriotism. A small crowd, including Emily, marched in a circle between the toy soldiers and the TV cameras. They all raised their fists each time they passed the cameras. The rest of the demonstrators waited. (Later, Susan recalled a man watching from an upstairs window in the Consulate. Perhaps that was another time, another place. Her memory for marches wasn't as clear as Emily's.) The sound truck arrived with giant amplifiers. The MC explained that the march had been a cooperative effort and that representatives of ten different groups would be speaking.

Susan checked her watch and decided to leave quietly. She didn't seek out Emily or her other feminist friends to say goodbye. She might have to explain that she was going home to cook supper. She walked briskly to the subway as the Evangelical for Social Action was shouting, "Nixon may have postponed the bombing of North Vietnam, but the South is experiencing more bombing . . . ." Susan knew, everybody knew, that the fires in Cambodia and Laos would rage long after any Vietnam treaty. This was just like the last march and the one before that.

Meanwhile, in the faraway land of power, Richard Nixon prepared for his million dollar inaugural ball. And in the faraway land of bombings, Indochinese women watched their children being ripped to shreds. Here in the land of official observers, Susan pretended to serve in the last peace march.

Dark Midnight

Damn organization won't pay your expenses to rent a car, so you have to wait 20 minutes in the drizzling dark for the Greyhound, penniless because the ticket clerk won't accept personal checks. Besides which, you have lost your tape recorder and you are surrounded in line by crew cuts on their way back to Fort Lewis. It will take hours to get to Olympia. It will take all the patience you have. You scramble for a seat up front, pull out your book and discover that the front seat has no reading lamp.

"So as not to blind the driver," says the woman next to you who is herself actually blind. Can you complain to a blind woman that you can't read in the dark? Learn braille, gringa.

"Travelling is such an opportunity," she is saying. "You can learn something from everyone." A business student, married to another blind business student.

You are listening.

"It's an apprenticeship program for IBM with almost guaranteed job placement. You don't know what that means for a blind person."

How does she know you are listening?

"It pays well, and we have a nice little apartment. Maybe we'll be able to have kids in a few years."

You want to ask her how she opens cans and fixes soup, let alone how she plans to raise children.

She reads your mind, skilled without lamps as she is. "Go ahead, ask questions if you like."

But you have run out of questions, even for the Governor tomorrow. Dreadful, leachy job, this lobbying.

"A lobbyist, how interesting," she says with polite curiosity as though she were talking to someone as fascinating as a repossessor of television sets.

"For what are you lobbying? That is the correct term, 'lobbying,' isn't it?"

You are silent, paralyzed by her voice. High-pitched. The key of a bottle bobbing against a buoy in the night sea.

"He's doing a fine job, I hear," she says to fill the void.

You know by this that she is a much nicer person than you, more considerate. But you're annoyed by her political naïveté. Doesn't she know about the cutbacks in social services?

"Oh, yes, that's very interesting," she says.

Interesting, shit lady, you think. It's crucial. The Governor is a practicing fundamentalist American. Taking money from social services and giving tax concessions to businesses like IBM. Why is she working for IBM? Just because she's blind, does that make it OK? Don't patronize her. Argue. You know you should argue, but you are too tired to find anything that will make sense.

You tell her, "yes, it's interesting."

The crew cuts have left and it's only twenty minutes to Olympia. Just enough time to make it to the hotel bar before it closes at 1:00 a.m. Just enough time to order a gin and tonic, take it up to your room and phone the Greyhound in Seattle to see if they've found your tape recorder at the fucking ticket counter. Thirty more minutes of conversation. Only seven years in this business and already you've run dry. To think that you chose this job because you liked talking to people.

"Thanks for the chat," she says sincerely. "If you don't mind, I'll just rest a while." She leans back on the headrest, her eyes wide open to the darkness.

"Yes," you say. "Sure."

Maybe you'll make it a double martini. The Governor's secretary better not cut the interview short. You pray, like you haven't prayed for anything in ages, that you make it to the hotel bar before 1:00 a.m.

IV

The Right Hand on the Day of Judgment

"What do you think of the piece from Zaragoza?" Susan asked. "Will you give me the OK? Can we count on Tony to keep his mouth shut?"

Harry shook his head, "I've been trying to decide just that, all morning."

Susan could never tell which was misshapen—Harry or his old gabardine suits. A proper Charlie Chaplin, he was, with manila envelopes and foolscap carbon sheets hanging out of his cracked brown leather briefcase. No, more like James Stewart playing the absent-minded diplomat, bumbling through social banalities, but driven by political commitment. He hadn't bothered to comb the grey wisps over his baldness this morning. She didn't know exactly how old Harry was. Somewhere in his late fifties, if he had fought in Spain.

"Remember Tony's antics in Uruguay," said Susan, "flaunting his press card. He was lucky to escape intact. We may be spending a lot of money for him to holiday in prison."

"Yes, yes," nodded Harry. "We probably should call him home now."

She played with the coffee bean beads hanging to the waist of her black pullover. The bean beads—being cheap, a tribute to the Brazilian Liberation Fund and still stylish—were among her more successful compromises to fashion. She concentrated on Harry's careful words.

"On the other hand," he watched her closely, "you have to take certain risks, like we did a couple of years ago with the coverage of Prague."

She released the beads and picked up her fountain pen.

Harry continued, "I supposed that's what journalistic courage is all about. To hell with it. Tell Tony to go ahead. I'll trust my instincts. By the way, thanks a lot for finishing up the layouts. You're my right hand. Don't know what I would do without you."

◇

Susan packed the solicitor's letters and her notes on South African sports in the frayed blue folder marked "Mockup." She listened to a muffled slam from the small front room. The office was gulping another person. It had felt stuffy lately, cramped. She never believed those gas fires were healthy.

◇

Hilary rang the next day, at the worst possible time. Into that damn consciousness raising trip. But she was so funny when she got sarcastic about Harry. Susan really wanted to laugh. Instead, she defended Harry, "Nonsense, Hilary. He's totally committed to the struggle. This paper is his life."

"Then he better start making funeral arrangements," said Hilary. "If *The Artisan* survives, it's your doing. You're responsible for organizing the mockup, for convincing the contributors to stick around, for getting Colson to reconsider publishing. Everyone knows it."

"Enough high drama," said Susan. "Sometimes I wonder how much you defend me just because I'm a woman. Anyway, *enough,* because I've got to get back to work."

"All right, kid. If things don't work out on TA, though, you know you've always got a job in Montreal. Take care of yourself. Cheers."

Susan hung up and turned to the secretary, "Alice, could you hold all the calls for twenty minutes?"

She spoke through the pots of drugged ferns. She hated that gas fire. If it did this to plants, what did it do to people? She stared past Alice, through the dingy window panes. The brick wall across the alley looked like the pointilism she had studied at the Art Gallery last term, the image was diffused, then discernible. She had been meaning to clean that window for months.

The flaccid blond woman nodded politely from inside her *National Enquirer,* looked up and smiled obligingly, "OK, Mrs. . . . I mean, Susan. I'll tell them you're in a meeting."

It had taken Alice six weeks to call her Susan. But who was she to talk? It had taken *her* four *months* to call Harry, Harry. (The same thing happened with her mother-in-law. It would have been so much easier if she had said, "Call me 'Mom,' or 'Mrs. Thompson,' or 'Ruth.' ") And he was characteristically indifferent the day she finally got up the nerve to say, "Harry, I think . . . ."

"We should work on the logo and the pages," she said as she entered his office, "if we're going to get them in by Friday, don't you think?"

"Yes, yes. And the solicitor's coming. Can you tie those things up for me. I've got some work to do on the censorship piece. Perhaps you could come in after lunch?"

"Sure, Harry."

◇

She got a good start and didn't want to break for lunch. When people asked Susan why she worked so hard she explained that in a dotty way, she believed in *The Artisan,* "Canada's radical literary forum." Their coverage of Indochina was closely read. She was proudest of the space they gave to trade union politics, to non-intellectuals, breaking down media exclusivity. She felt like she was helping to change things, not directly, but by being a resource for people who could.

Harry didn't buzz her that afternoon. Just as well because she had to work into the evening editing. Harry hated multiple reviews, but she was glad she had suggested juxtaposing the books on Canadian and Irish nationalism. Anyway, he would like the critiques of *The Female Eunuch.* The writer showed how women's liberation was a bourgeois deviation from class struggle. If they continued all this nitpicking about who ran meetings, nothing would get done. Hilary would scream "Leftist chauvinism," but Susan agreed with the article. What was wrong with complimenting a man's work at home or in the office, if it were all part of the same struggle? What was wrong with typing, for instance? It had been her entree to university politics where she met Guy and into TA, itself.

The telephone resonated in the empty room. She hesitated. She didn't want to get home late again.

"Señor Harry Simpson, por favor."

"I'm sorry," she scrambled for her California Spanish, "Señor Simpson no está aqui."

"OK, Susan," a Canadian voice broke in. "I'm glad I caught you."

The operator faded in a garble of Spanish. "This is Tony Sanchez. I've got a great lead. Marquez is briefing a few journalists in the hills above Zaragoza. I need more money and time if I'm going to cover it."

"I'll get Harry on the phone tonight and we'll see."

"No, no time for that. The MULA are taking a small group of us today. They're leaving in an hour. I need to know right away whether I can have $200 in expenses and four more days on the deadline. If I don't go with them now, I'll never get into camp."

"Give me forty-five minutes to reach Harry."

"Thirty-five."

"Right, call me back in thirty-five minutes on the 06 line."

She didn't think Harry could refuse an exclusive interview with Marquez. The number was busy. But then, Harry was so reticent about the Trots. Susan dialed his number again. Busy. And again. She would never make it to Harry's house in Rosedale and back in that time. However, Guy could. Her only option was to ring Guy.

"Susan, hon, where the hell are you?"

"I'm afraid I'm still at work. Something's come up. An

emergency call from Spain. Tony has a chance to go to Marquez' camp, but we have to reach him with the OK in a half-hour. I'll explain later. Could you do me a huge favor? I can't get Harry on the phone. Could you drive over there and tell him to call me here?"

"Well, I don't know. I have my doubts about Marquez' position. The caucus was discussing just this afternoon that his kind of nationalism is . . . "

"Oh, come on Guy. We can't ignore a movement as big as that."

"Fucking hell, it's not as if I don't have enough to do tonight, preparing the caucus platform, finding time to work on my thesis."

"Guy, look, I'm sorry to impose. But this could mean the survival of TA."

"What about the survival of something euphemistically known as 'our marriage'?"

She told him she also believed in healthy confrontations, that they should both get into their feelings about the marriage, but couldn't it wait an hour until she got home?

When she hung up, the only remorse she felt was from her Yoga teacher's lecture on back tension. How had she taken Guy's abuse for so long? His rambling accusations as he peered into the aquarium feeding his black bullheads and veiltails. The phone rang and she answered it with relief.

"Susan? Harry here. What's all this about a Spanish Revolution?"

She repeated the story.

"I'll have to think about it."

"But there's no time to think about it. Tony's calling back in twenty minutes."

"Why did you arrange a fool thing like that? This is a big decision. We risk a huge hole. On the other hand, a good piece could swing Colson's judgment."

"Yes, yes," she said. "But we've got to make a decision."

"Don't pressure me," he said. "I'll call you back."

"OK, Harry, but please remember to call within fifteen minutes."

Had she been too hyper? Guy always said she got hyper in emergencies. Better to get hyper than paralyzed like Harry. Three minutes to nine. TA's survival could hinge on one good story. She tried to ring Harry. The number was busy. All right, she thought, he must be calling back. She waited, weighted by silence. Finally the phone rang. It was the 06 line. It was Tony.

"Go ahead with it, Tony. Where do you want the money wired?"

She gave him three extra days for the deadline. Elated, she was also surprised at her confidence and her indifference to Harry. He could call her at home if he wanted to find out what had happened. She put on her raincoat and gathered several manuscripts into her briefcase.

Susan walked briskly to the bus stop. Usually she let herself be sucked home on the subway. She hated how people in the underground corridors rushed unconsciously past each other, like numbers in the formulas of some ironic computer programmer. The subway was part of her mindless survival in Toronto. (By the time she jostled a seat, arranged the groceries and briefcase on her lap, she was too exhausted to exhale the parentheses with which she had ordered her day.) Tonight she saw a bus as soon as she turned the corner. She clinked 15 cents into the news vendor's tin, picked up a *Toronto Star* and hailed the wheezing, swaggering wagon.

◇

Guy wasn't home. He probably stopped off at the Brunswick after Harry's. She just wanted to forget the whole mess. She tidied up the living room and went into the kitchen to make Guy's sandwiches. She always made them at night because he hated the smell of mustard in the morning. She left him a note before crawling under the covers. The shadow of his body became noticeable in the first light. She hadn't heard him come back. She must have slept well. She left the room silently at 8:00 a.m.

◇

"Mr. Simpson had to leave for Winnipeg unexpectedly," Alice said quickly. "He told me that I was to refer any calls to you. He said you would understand about the Manitoba piece, interviewing Dr. Wolfe and all. He said he would call you."

Susan didn't understand and Harry didn't call. Her worries about the Spanish piece disappeared under the havoc of a dozen other decisions about type face and photographs and cartoons. She didn't have time to panic. Occasionally she would notice herself making decisions and then review her work peripherally.

The review of the Greer book still bothered her. Somehow it wasn't conclusive enough. She called Hilary for some information, knowing full well that it was a terrible risk.

Hilary exploded. "Sure, sure there are a lot of problems with 'feminist analysis,' but Greer doesn't represent the whole Women's Movement. Just like every bourgeois black prick doesn't represent African Liberation."

"Oh, come on, Hilary, you can't possibly compare the oppression of women to the exploitation of the Third World. That's going pretty far." Susan caught herself almost shouting down the line and said finally, "Look, I've got to get back to work."

The next two days accelerated with the pressure of deadline against Harry's loose editing. She grew more and more annoyed with him until she realized that she was being unfair. Harry must be distracted, somehow. Normally, he was a fine editor, the most political person she knew. He had gone through so much with the Communist Party in the 50's. No wonder he was a bit threadbare.

When he sauntered in the office on Monday, Susan settled for a modest admonition, "Harry, you know I had to make a decision about the Spanish piece."

"The Spanish . . . oh, yes. I tried to call you back, but I was interrupted. Then Ethel made some emergency call. Sorry about that. I reckoned you were perfectly sensible. What did you tell him?"

"To take three extra days on the story. And I wired $150 expenses."

"Fine. Just fine," he said as he walked into his office. He stuck his head back out the door, "Oh, I do have some questions about those columns in the front of the paper. And about the multiple review. I've told you before that this isn't an academic journal. I suppose it's too late now," he sighed. "Could you stop by the office on the way back from the printer's tonight? I've got to talk over the publicity with you."

"Gosh, I'm sorry Harry, but I promised Guy a real supper tonight. It's our anniversary." She tried to rationalize the sentimentality, but before she could come up with something that might satisfy Harry, he said, "Neither of us will be able to afford supper if this mockup isn't approved. Come on. I promise to give you a couple of days off at the end of this thing."

Damn him. She wasn't some functionary scurrying after a Christmas bonus. What did he think she was doing while he was in Winnipeg? Hang on. She would sound like Hilary in a minute. The publicity did have to be done. Hang on, Susan. Watch out for the bourgeois individualism.

They met for two hours that evening. She briefed him on last week's decisions. He reassured her that she had done as well as he could have.

◇

Guy was furious. He was having a hard enough time doing his research lately. When he borrowed a few hours to spend with her, she could at least show up. As far as he could see, she was ALWAYS having emergencies and he wondered, he just wondered without being too analytical about it, how many of them were escapes from their shitty relationship. Since she didn't seem to find the occasion so portentous, he was going back to study and would return when dinner was ready. He wished her Happy Anniversary, by the way.

Salad making always soothed her. When she was little, she imagined the best part of being married was going to be sitting

in a blue-tiled kitchen reaching into the cornucopia for another
cucumber. She liked to score the cucumbers on the edges
with a fork so that when she cut them, they came out as un-
predictably as paper dolls. (She and Guy were the best of
their generation, the archetype virile revolutionaries who
might be Mr. and Mrs. American in another era, she mused.
Smart, confident, committed. He would finish his Ph.D. in
psychology and they would take up his post in Havana. She
would raise their kids in a healthy workers' state. But the
order seemed to be breaking down. Susan wasn't sure she
wanted to quit her job. Guy had let his thesis drag on for
another year. He never *did* anything overt to annoy her—
that's why she felt it was her fault—it was what he *didn't* do.
She couldn't count on him for everything. In the end, he
didn't even do his own work. Maybe she put too much pressure on him.) Tomatoes were satisfying when they were fresh
and firm like these. She hated the overripe ones that sagged
under the knife and squirted messily over the glistening chop-
ping board. Raw mushrooms were the best, falling into thin,
porous slices like wafers of fungus. Lettuce could be tedious
when it was too wet. (She felt like a real bitch sometimes.
She had to *pry* to learn what happened during his day. The
conversation would be like an oral exam with halting, circum-
spect replies. Sometimes his withdrawal was an ambush. Like
that weekend of the Third World Medical Conference. He insisted he wanted to go. Then on Thursday he announced that
he still hadn't fixed the thermostats in the monkey room—on
Thursday! Her work schedule was ruined for two weeks. It
was only afterwards that she realized she might have gone
alone.) Susan carefully dried the leaves until they looked like
the heavy green tissue paper she used for collages when she
was in Sister Matthew's art class. Fun, all this cutting and re-
assembling. That's what she liked best—putting it all in order.
She detested random salads, crisp stews in smudged glass
bowls. First she put in bits of lettuce then the celery, onion,
mushrooms. She sprinkled rosemary and basil. On top she
wheeled the tomatoes and cucumbers. (Guy would under-

stand once they had a chance to sit down and discuss the chaos at work. To be fair, she hadn't told him very much yet. She always got home so late. After she cooked and cleaned up and they watched the news, there wasn't much time to talk.) The chops were sizzling and the potatoes were done just the way he liked them, with the jackets falling off.

"Guy," she called into the living room. "Guy."

No answer, so she set the hot plates on the stove and looked in. "Guy," she said gently. He was asleep at his desk, his head on a new Asimov science fiction book. "Guy," she said compassionately. This petulant boy was her protector and partner for life? "Guy," she said bitterly. She couldn't cope with the anger. She didn't know where to release it—at him—or at her own poor judgment. "This is our anniversary," she told herself. She thought about the layouts she had to do tonight. She shook him, "Harry," she said and stopped. How often she had almost said that? Eerie. How often she had mixed them up in dreams. And once, when she had promised Guy to deposit the grant in his checking account, she had put it in Harry's instead. She had felt like such an idiot when the teller showed her the numbers were different.

Guy looked up, "Who did you call?"

"Sorry, love, I'm always incoherent when I'm tired."

"Well, I'm tired too. I think I'll push off to bed."

"But you haven't eaten. And it's our anniversary."

"I suppose you should have thought about both those items a little earlier. I'm worn out. See you in the morning." He stumbled up from his swivel chair, almost knocking over the half-empty bottle of sherry. She hungrily regarded the level, a sufficient ablution for guilt. She was grateful they still shared some things.

◇

Susan woke late with a terrible hangover. Not so much an alcoholic headache as a residue of remorse. She rose immediately, careful not to awaken Guy. She saw herself gazing into

43

a cup of black coffee. Running to the subway. Answering the phones. What was she doing in Toronto?

"Hello, Susan. This is Hilary. Got a news bulletin for you. Colson is coming down. Thought I should warn you that I got carried away with him yesterday. He was expounding on the vigour and genius of one Harry Simpson."

What had Hilary done with her big mouth now?

"Well, you know, kid, I'm not thoroughly indiscreet. I didn't let on that Harry was an absolute moron."

Susan didn't know what to blame more—Harry's fraudulence or her own complicity. How long did she think she could play innocent minion?

"What did you say to Colson?" Susan asked.

"Not much. I just dropped a few hints about Harry's long sojourn away from the office and about his banker's hours. I reckoned that the rest was up to you."

Susan rang off. She buzzed Harry's office, "Harry, I've got to talk with you."

"Sure, sure," he said. "And would you bring in those readership surveys? Also the circulation reports. Colson has decided to catch us off guard. This could mean the end of TA if we're not prepared."

She watched him take notes on her work. He tried, at first, to comprehend; by noon he was grasping for details. Harry hadn't made a straightforward decision in months. Lately he had been fading out around deadline time. She always made her decisions sound like clerical minutae. At the end of today's session, she told Harry that she wanted to be in on the conference with Colson. He was surprised, then agreed with alacrity. "Of course, of course." It was a sensible idea.

◇

The next morning, the fragrant and glossy mockup arrived an hour before Colson was due. Susan was quite proud of the classy logo, the solid articles, the lively layout. It was so perfectly formed. And after last night, she might have to resign herself to this kind of posterity. She and Guy had never had such a row. It was more like a schism although it was about the same old issues. He charging that she spent too much time at her work; she retorting that he felt jealous because he couldn't do his own work. He said she would have to make a choice, decide what she wanted. Susan said she didn't know what she wanted and went to bed. Now she was redeemed from all that by the new magazine. So excited about Colson's visit, she could hardly concentrate on the circulation figures.

Harry buzzed her on the intercom, "It looks great. Just great. Just what I had imagined. I really couldn't have done it without you."

In the middle of the morning, a heavily cologned man wearing a grey striped suit lumbered into the office.

"Harry Simpson, please," he said, leaning heavily on her desk.

Before she had time to explain that Harry Simpson had a meeting this morning, the man added, "My name is Colson. Carl Colson. I think Harry's expecting me." He pulled a wrinkled handkerchief from his back pocket and wiped his forehead. "Terrible stairs. Ever think of getting a lift installed?"

This was the visionary publisher? They had been trying to impress this man for three months? He was going to judge *The Artisan?* Susan hadn't expected Leon Trotsky, but . . . .

"Just one moment, please," she heard herself assuming the respect she wanted to give him. How hollow did her voice sound? How disappointed did her face look? She watched him thanking her, taking a chair, smiling at her. She supposed she was smiling at him.

"Carl, Carl, welcome," Harry thrust his hand at Carl Colson. "Sorry, I had no idea you were waiting. How long have they kept you here?" Harry ushered him inside. Susan waited demurely for her invitation, but Harry didn't even turn around to nod before he shut the door.

"Well, well," she heard him say to Colson, "What do you think of my baby? How about the logo, eh?"

She could not bear the sound of them sitting in the large office congratulating each other. She went out to wash her face. When she came back, she was still flushed. Her copy of the magazine was gone.

"They've taken it in," said Alice delicately. "They said they didn't want anything to happen to it."

What goddam arrogance. It was her sweat. What absolute gall!

Susan heard the intercom buzz.

Always too hyper, Susan said to herself, always too hyper. Hell, they had probably expected her to follow them into Harry's office. Perhaps she should just go in now and save the formality of answering the line. No, she would wait for them to ask her. They owed her that much.

"Susan, I was wondering if you could do us a favor?"

"Sure, I'll be right in."

"No need to trouble yourself. Could you just ask Alice— her line seems to be jammed—could you just ask Alice to bring us two cups of sugared tea?"

"Sure, Harry, sure."

She relayed the message and watched Alice prepare the tea, place the cups on a tray with some chocolate digestives and take it in. Now Susan felt nothing but the pure release of acrimony. She was too angry to be intimidated, too angry even to be restrained by any kind of judgment. Susan went over and banged on Harry's door.

She was greeted by an astonished Alice, carrying an empty tray in one hand and a stack of file folders in the other. Susan smiled at her and walked into the office.

"I've finished my work for the morning, Harry. I'd like to sit in now."

"Yes, yes, Mrs. Thompson," said Colson expansively. "Do come in. Harry tells me you're such a bright girl, with real drive." Colson brightened, "Harry says you're his right hand."

"Sorry to inform you about the amputation."

"I beg your pardon?" asked Colson, his frown crossing grotesquely with the receding joviality.

"This girl's got a great sense of humor, Carl, just one of the things I haven't had a chance to tell you about her," Harry smiled indulgently.

Susan looked at him seriously. "I'm thinking about leaving the paper, Harry, about going to a job in Montreal unless some changes are made."

Harry was still.

"But, but," said Colson. "This is a silly time for that, my love. I mean just when *The Artisan* has been reborn. This mockup is brilliant. And to think we were all so afraid of failure."

"And of success," she said.

"What was that, my dear?"

"Listen, this mockup is a good start, but only that. We could have much more direct reporting from Latin America and Southern Africa; a broader review policy . . . ." She knew she wasn't talking to either of them, but just enjoying the rush of her own voice. "Some hard investigative pieces and wider circulation in the West."

"That's all very well, but hang on, girl, and look for a moment at what Harry's accomplished here. The multiple review is superb. The Spanish piece is a real coup."

Susan had no reason, no inclination to expose Harry. He and Colson would find out about each other soon enough.

She said, "Look, I'll outline the ideas. You can think about them. If you feel they make sense, I'll stay and help. If you don't, I've got another job."

Susan and Colson turned to Harry who looked terribly tired.

"Yes," Harry said. "They're sensible ideas. Perhaps we could discuss them after lunch?"

"Well, well," answered Colson. "Of course we're open to change. Just look at this issue, real revolutionary editing."

"I know," said Susan. She picked up her copy of *The Artisan* and went back to her desk. "See you after lunch," she said as she closed the door on them.

Newsworthy

John Forester, 59, of 18993 Montez Drive, Walnut Creek, reported that his wife, Gertrude, 62, was missing on Tuesday. He had not seen her since Saturday night when the couple attended a performance of *The Marriage of Figaro* at the Opera House in San Francisco.

Forester, an insurance salesman, said that his wife had been calm and collected throughout the performance. Afterwards, they stopped for coffee at the Yum Yum Room. Mrs. Forester went to the lavatory and did not return.

Forester said his wife had shown no signs of worry lately. Two months ago, she had mentioned divorce, but apparently became reconciled after a long talk and a visit with the family doctor. Mrs. Forester, an active volunteer at their church and a local hospital, has no past record of instability. (Picture, page five.)

V

Stray

Susan felt like the stray cat from *In Our Time* as she sat shivering in the parlor of the dark rooming house on Admiral Road. Outside the yellowed lace curtains snow flurried with relentless delicacy. The parlor was heated by an electric fire. This Edwardian contraption provided an illusion of warmth as a light wheel circled under translucent plastic coals. Watching the prism turn, she tried to time the colors against the urgent balance piece of the marble mantle clock.

"Far out light show, eh?"

He was a freak. Blond ponytail. Splotchy hiking boots. Fatigued jacket. Susan wondered if they played acid rock here all night long. Probably no one in this rooming house sleeps after midnight, she thought. Probably they'll think I'm some sort of Miss Priscilla.

"Yeah, it almost keeps you warm," she bluffed composure. "Say, do you know when Robert is coming back?"

"You can never tell about Robert," laughed the handsome young man. He's the busiest absentee landlord in the Annex. But look, here's the switch for the fire," he knelt down gracefully. "All you've got so far is the light show. This is how you turn on the heating filaments."

"My name's, uh, uh, Susan," she said, blushing.

"I'm Phil. Musta been a hard day, Susan."

She nodded and looked down at her lap to hide the blushing.

"How about a cup of camomile tea?"

"Right on," she said, realizing this was not Phil's dialect. He was more cooled out. Laid back. She felt auntish, the way she always felt with hippies. Always so much older. And consequently younger—as if she hadn't lived through anything. Virginal. She hadn't made the trips. She had stayed home and worked.

"What do you do?" she heard herself saying. The wrong question. Why was she so obsessed with what people did? Bourgeois bitch. Was she messing up on purpose to prove that she wasn't capable of living with hippies?

He handed her a cracked mug of tea, baptism after the *mea culpa*.

"Depends on where you're coming from," Phil was saying. "I do music. I do meditation. I do boxes."

"Boxes?"

"In a packing plant up on Dupont, loading boxes of gears to be sent down to Buffalo."

"What sort of music?" she asked, enjoying the gentle tea. She had never liked camomile before. Next time she would remember not to use sugar.

"I listen to what I play," he rubbed the stick pointing out of his back pocket.

"A flautist. Wow." "Flautist" was definitely wrong. "Wow" sounded OK.

"And you?" he asked. "You look like a pretty classy lady to be moving into one of Big Bob's half-refinished houses. You break up with your husband or something?"

"Does it show on my face?" Susan asked, stricken.

"On your hands," he smiled.

The ring mark was visible, whiter than Ontario winter, and her hands were shaking, despite the warm mug.

"I'm kind of worried," she said, "about, about . . . my cat. She's only a little thing. I just got her. I mean I just found her. A stray. Does he mind?"

"Roberto? You bet. He hates all animals and other living things. You'd never be able to hide her. The vacant room is next to his. And he's got a nose like a narc dog."

She lowered her eyes. The hands. Her damn hands. Three hands. He was massaging her knuckles.

"But my room is in the attic," he said quietly. "Good for flute playing. Good for hiding strays."

Phil's smile of conspiracy now turned to greeting as a tall man entered the kitchen.

"Robert, this is Susan, our new housemate."

"So you've seen the room and it's OK?" Robert asked, only mildly surprised.

"No, not exactly," she said.

But of course she would take it, despite the broken concrete floor and the water-stained wallpaper. She would take it for her stray cat.

◇

Phil happened to be around the evening she moved in. He offered to help her carry the boxes.

"Thanks, but I can do it on my own," she said.

"Boxes," he reminded her. "I'm an expert on boxes."

"Thank you," she said, resigned to his kindness.

First he carried the perforated shoe box up to the attic. Then the boxes of books to the second floor. "All these books," he exclaimed. "Too heavy"? she asked. "No, he did this all day, remember, boxes? But *so many*. When did she find time to relax?"

"Intellectuals get uptight relaxing," interrupted Mandy from the second floor landing. She introduced herself as a "radikeel med student," explaining she always tried to forget most of what she learned right after the exam. She said she was into med school for the nitrous oxide. She would catch them later, after her anatomy lab test.

Susan also met Christine, melting down the mahogany stairway in a long black skirt and a pink satin bed jacket. Phil had told her that Christine was a lesbian, that she read Tarot cards and made papier-mâché puppets. Christine smiled demurely and Susan could see she wasn't one of the dyke feminists, but more the Natalie Barney type. She had read a lot about lesbians this year.

Suddenly Susan felt like Sister Joseph Marie on a missionary field assignment. She was wearing a perfectly acceptable —even wrinkled—work shirt, and jeans. But she was sure they could all see through to her starched habits.

This was a new experience, a growth situation, as Guy would say in his own earnest, tedious way. She would learn a lot. She might learn how not to be straight. Hip? Mellow? She might at least learn the vocabulary.

"I hope you'll like it here," Phil said as he fixed the tea. "You and . . . .?"

She was confused, blushing at her confusion.

"Our refugee?" he asked.

"Oh, my cat's name is Imogene." Her laughter was the only visible trembling until she closed the door to her room.

Lying on the paisley floor pillow, she pulled Carol's old purple sleeping bag over herself. Just fine. She had had enough of beds for a while. Beds with embroidered pillowcases and floral sheets. Making their bed had been like laying a goddamn altar. This was simple, comfortable, easy to convert. She hated excess. Comfortable. Two in the morning. Comfortable, but she couldn't sleep. She ran through the projects in her mind. The layout was done. The darkroom time was scheduled. She could easily have the paste-up finished by tomorrow. Yes, work was fine. She and Hilary would go to the National Ballet on Saturday night. Sunday, she would take the yoga class. Letters. Maybe a good read, listening to the Pachelbel *Canon*. Sleep. She tried to remember the gigue after the *Canon*. Sleep, she whispered gently. Everything was settled. Why couldn't she sleep? What did acid rock sound like anyway?

The sherry was just for hospitality, she scolded herself as she poured a glass now. Probably shouldn't have bought it. She had passed by Brights three times that day. She didn't buy it for herself, more for a cordiality to friends. She would reassure her visitors that this new home was a civilized place, not a soiled old rooming house three blocks from wino land.

A spare, but civilized refuge. She had stored the marriage accessories in Robert's damp basement: her linens, the unbreakable dinnerware and the silver chafing dishes. She felt like an immigrant. Like her mother and Rosa Kaburi. The bottle of sherry would ease the transition. If someone dropped by, she would feel less like an evacuee and more like a passenger on an ocean liner—temporarily, voluntarily homeless. A traveler.

"This is the day of my liberation." She poured another sherry.

The woody sweetness of Guy's parents' living room used to encompass her after one glass of their Bristol Cream. Sherry was one part of the Thompson legacy she would keep. The only alcohol her mother ever drank was cans of Budweiser from the fridge. Sour. Urine before it made its own. Sherry would lend Susan a certain elegance, an immunity.

"This is the day of my liberation." All evening she had been telling herself how immune she was. "This is the day of my liberation." A claim. "This is the day of my liberation." A litany. Without an amen.

So what had she sacrificed with the divorce? Their move to Cuba had become a pipe dream. Children she could have with someone else. Or on her own. Hilary was right. What a fixation to think you needed to have a man to have a child.

Ruth Thompson had been as sweet as her woodened sherry the last time they spoke. "I'm so sorry," her mother-in-law had sighed. "I had no idea you children were having troubles. Yes, probably it *is* wise to part, for a while. What will you ever do with all your things? The silver? Oh, no, don't send it back. That sounds so permanent." (Susan knew, deep down, that Ruth liked her. Once, after two hours of civilized sherry, Ruth had told Susan she admired, maybe even envied her independence.) "Well, all right, send it back if that makes you happier. I'll keep it here for you. Yes, yes, we shall continue to write."

Now, pouring herself a second glass—the *last* glass, she promised—Susan lay back down on the paisley pillow. "Do this in remembrance of me," she thought foggily. How im-

pressed she had been when Guy told her that four generations
of his family had attended Berkeley. That he had relatives,
ancestors and descendants in the state legislature. A half-
million dollar vineyard harvested into a two million dollar
shopping center. Sherry in the parlor. Women confined in
the needlepoint. The first afternoon she had alone with Ruth,
they spent tranquillizing the poodles so they could be clipped.

Still, there had been security as a Thompson. There had
always been that security with Guy, before there was anything
else and after there was nothing else.

◇

Someone was sitting outside her window the next morning,
in the maple tree. Susan thought it was the telephone man at
first. She felt relieved because they had promised to install
the line yesterday and she really couldn't work without a telephone. Then she noticed that the cat was under his arm.
Shaking herself into morning, she realized it was Phil. He
rapped lightly on the window and she let him in.

"You looked like the telephone man," she said stupidly.

"More like a cat burglar, eh?"

They both laughed.

"We got on real well last night," Phil said. "She snuggled
right up to me. I left the window open. Must have gone out
to stalk zebra in the night 'cause when I woke up, there she
was, shivering out on a limb. Say," he touched Susan's bare
shoulder, "so are you."

The window was still open and it was starting to snow. She
was wearing a summer nightgown. He asked if he could join
her under the sleeping bag. She breathed deeply and nodded,
repeating to herself, "This is the day of my liberation."

◇

The second time that morning she was wakened by the telephone man. The doorbell rang downstairs. A knock on her
door. A loud voice. "Telephone man."

"Got to get to work, man," Phil yawned sleepily. "You
can put Imogene in my room when you leave the house. The

54

window's closed now."

After that, she went up often to visit the little stray. She insisted on maintaining separate quarters, relishing the security of her own room. During the day she went to *The Artisan;* afterwards she usually had a meeting. He was steady at his packing plant job and spent evenings with his flute and Imogene in the attic. Late at night, he would float into her room, shut off the ceiling lamp and light one of his sandalwood candles. So they came together in the dark and on weekends in High Park.

How she was touched by the compliments from this ponytailed freak. Susan had always been embarrassed, helpless about her straightness. (Such was the dowry from parochial school. Better on discipline than décolleté. When she graduated from St. Mary's, she couldn't understand the difference between mix n' match. Even now, in her jeans, she looked like an unfaded ingénue. Her Levis were zipped when everyone else's were buttoned.) Phil thoroughly enjoyed being her tutor. With him, she heard her first Procol Harum, ate her first hashcake and came close to taking acid.

◇

"How are you doing, dear?" Susan's mother phoned from California, ever hopeful of redeeming her back to civilization.

"Mellow," Susan said, inhaling a joint and reaching over to stroke Phil's thigh.

"Beg pardon," her mother said.

"Fine," Susan said, remembering the old language, assuming her former, solid voice, her cheerful daughter tone. "Did I tell you about my cat?"

◇

Susan began to understand how much of her generation she had missed. In college, she had no time between her cafeteria job and her studying for the Grateful Dead or Big Sur. She read *Rolling Stone* once, for a journalism class. She visited Haight Ashbury twice, taking out-of-town relatives on Sunday afternoons to view the hippies. Marriage had been a worthy sequel, working every night, reading together on Saturdays. (They tried earnestly to learn about Canada, another guilt to expiate. Not only were they white, middle-class and heterosexual, but they were American.) Perhaps that was what was wrong with marriage. Perhaps it was just too straight.

Although Phil had never read *The Artisan,* he said if that's how she spent her time, he wanted to see a copy. He didn't get beyond the last couple of pages. He always read from the back. They had some good talks about the office and he stopped making women's lib jokes after a while.

"Watch it," she had said, "I'm serious about feminism."

"I can see that" he laughed, adding, "politics is cool."

"Politics is not *cool,*" she said.

He couldn't handle the dialectic.

"I know you'd agree with me if we discussed it," she said. But he didn't feel like it.

So she accepted a moratorium on socialism, feminism and the counterculture because she was *tired* of figuring things out. She wrote to her friends that he was a nice guy, a natural non-sexist. They had no struggles about authority or fucking or washing the dishes.

◇

"We can still be friends, can't we?" Guy telephoned to ask. "I thought we might get together."

"Sure," she said, out of guilt, holding the cat close to her cheek.

"The abortion," he said abruptly. "We never really talked about it. You made that decision, you know. I want to deal with that. I feel I'm still mourning . . . ."

"Friends," she spoke absently, wistfully, directly into the cat's eyes.

"Don't get ironic with me, Susan. I'm just trying to be open with you."

◇

Sometimes Phil talked about a muse in Afghanistan, a spiritual leader, but she did not press him about it. Whenever he talked about leaving, he promised he would bequeath her the half-melted sandalwood candles, a collection of Blind Faith, a finely polished cheroot and one of his flutes.

He wasn't a very good flautist. And whenever *she* thought of leaving *him,* it was because she didn't really like his music.

It would be up to the cat to choose between them.

Someone Else's Baby

The Food Coop met every Saturday morning at ten. Ted waved to Maureen as she parked her bike. He was armed with someone else's baby, a kid who was being raised in his commune.

Maureen helped him weigh the tomatoes.

"We broke up a couple of weeks ago," he told her. "It was Maryanna's decision. I still don't get it. She claims there isn't anyone else. What did I do?"

Maureen shrugged and tried to look sympathetic. Ted was all right for a man—gentle and pretty unoppressive. "Maybe Maryanna just wanted to be alone."

"But we had so many plans."

Maureen was glad he didn't notice her brief smile.

He explained all he could explain. "I told her she could sleep with anyone she wanted. I even offered to introduce her to this new guy at the Institute. You know I've always been a supporter of women's liberation."

Maureen inched over to get some hazelnuts before they were all gone.

"Why couldn't we work it out together? We're still the same people we were four years ago. I *do not* get it. It's happening to so many of our friends. Marni and Joe. Chris and Peter. The women are leaving. And, yeah, you left Mort. It was the same with you." He tried not to look accusing.

She nodded.

"Listen, it would really help to talk about this some time," he said. "How about dinner next Friday?"

"Can't Friday," she said.

He shifted the baby higher on his hip.

"And it wasn't exactly the same with me." She secured the basket to the back of her bicycle. "I mean I decided to be a lesbian."

He fell silent for a moment.

"See you next Saturday morning," he said. He told the baby to wave good-bye, because now, both his arms were full.

VI

Single Exposure

Susan was sitting alone in the quiet restaurant, leafing through *The Four-Gated City* for her place. She moved the candle closer. Perfect. Or as near to it as anything in the last three days. The redwood panelling reminded her of restaurants on Fisherman's Wharf—that and the kitsch fishnets with the colored glass balls. At the rate of service around here, the waiter may have gone to San Francisco for the fish.

Ever since Susan had moved to England last year, she had planned to come to Cornwall. Was it a silly Arthurian romance to hike along the cliffs in early winter? Susan had counted on and dreaded the trip. She needed the time alone to think and to work on the book, but she was afraid she would be lonely. The first two mornings had been hell—long and steep. Today hadn't been so tough.

The door opened with a draft and three men arguing. The short one blurted anxiously. "I didn't mean to lay an authoritarian trip on you about the time." After a long, rather ceremonial debate, they took the table next to Susan.

She opened her pendant watch—eight o'clock. Where was the bloody waiter? She had to get back to her room and plan the shots for tomorrow. Pushing the menu obviously off to the edge of the table, she returned to Lessing.

"Oh, excuse me, Miss, are you dining alone?" asked a short Englishman.

What the hell did he think she was doing, eating with the ghost of her mother? Oh, dear, why was she so touchy? Just a friendly question. And she knew her role—amiable, no-nonsense American.

"Yeah, I'm on my own." she said.

"Would you care to join us, then?" She heard an upper-class Oxbridge accent. "I do hate to see people dining alone," he said.

She admitted that they were reasonable looking: three men in their mid-twenties, blue jeans and Shetland sweaters. Bright, but slightly self-conscious from the edge of their Laing and Lorenz conversation. Damnit, she was happy alone with her book. She regarded him closely. A simple invitation; no need to elucidate. She found nothing in his face except subtle charm, not even discomfort at waiting for the reply. She decided she wouldn't mind some company for a couple of hours.

"Let me introduce myself. I am Andre and I'm from London. This is Colin, a true Scot and a dedicated nationalist." He indicated a thin, skittish man. "And Ronald, next to you. One of your countrymen, I suspect."

"I thought I heard an American accent," she said, hating herself immediately. Expatriates were such archetype Americans. Businessmen on assignment overseas and students searching out their roots in theses. Or they were as confused as she was—exasperated by the compromises of American politics; guilty about deserting the States; ambivalent about their positions in England. She hated the clubbishness of Americans who sipped Tom Collins' or smoked Oaxacan hash and griped about England's primitive indoor heating.

"What part of America are you from?" asked Ronald.

"San Francisco," she said, wincing to herself at the word "America."

"Isn't it imperialist to say 'America'?" interrupted Colin. "You don't own the whole bloody continent. Yet."

She liked Colin.

"You'll have to excuse our sarcasm," said Andre. "It's because . . . ."

"Because of the weekend," Ronald nodded solemnly. "Let's be up front."

"Because of the weekend," agreed Andre. "You see, we've all been on a Gestalt encounter at St. Ives. Trying to dispel the cognitive fog around our emotions." He reached inside his red parka and pulled out a brochure, *Deep Life Diving Off The Cornish Coast.*

Susan glanced courteously at the seminar topics.

Ronald explained. "We each wanted to reconsider our priorities, if you know what I mean. We had life all tallied up, but forgot to account for our *feelings*. It was, well, 'passionless.' A few months ago, I wouldn't have been able to say 'passionless.' Do you understand?"

Did she understand? Could she relate? Would she empathize? She had always tried before. She had been through this so often with the same character—the aging young professional who suddenly discovers that the missing ingredient is passion. So he practices spontaneity. He lets his receding hair grow past his ears and has it styled in the androgyne salon. He buys desert boots and work shirts and goes to Truffaut films. He espouses women's liberation because no one should be afraid of flying. He eats yogurt for dessert and takes honey in his coffee to be good to his body in hopes that some lady will notice and be good to it too.

"The dichotomy is very well expressed in *Equus*," said Andre.

"But isn't it a little forced, there?" said Susan. Caught now, she realized she had done the same therapy and attended the same plays. She was very relieved when a fresh young man in a blue linen jacket interrupted them. "May I serve you a wine?"

"That sounds super," said Ronald. "But not South African."

"Or Chilean," said Andre. "I don't care if it was made before the coup. How about Mateus? That's safe now, thank god, and it tastes decent. Mateus rosé? A nice political-culinary compromise?"

"Not if you follow the MPLA line," said Colin.

She regarded them soberly. Trying to keep a straight face, she offered, "And not the Spanish if you consider the Basques. Nor the Greek, if you read Theodorakis' statement last night. So why don't we forget the whole thing and have beer? Here's to conscienced alcoholism." They did not laugh.

Returning with a tray of Tartan cans, the confused waiter inquired tentatively, "And your dinner order?"

"I'll have moules marinières to begin," said Andre. "And the lobster. That is local, isn't it?"

"Yes sir," said the waiter, pleased to find someone who ordered normally.

"Pommes au gratin and brussels sprouts." He glanced with momentary regret at the wine list and then nodded graciously to Susan. "I hope you don't mind my going first. One assumes it's the proper thing to do in these days of increasing feminist sensibility."

Sounded like some kind of plague, this feminist sensibility. Relax, she told herself, and resolved to be less sardonic.

"Well, now, Susan. How long are you here for?" asked Ronald. "On vacation? Alone?"

"Yes," she said. "I'm on a working holiday."

"Oh, for how long?" smiled Colin.

"About a fortnight."

"A walking holiday," said Ronald, mishearing her. "How sensible. Amazing how fleshy we get. Where are you walking?"

"Bus to Land's End tomorrow," she said. "I'm walking to St. Just."

"Hey, why don't you join us?" asked Ronald.

◇

She woke five minutes late the next morning, zipped into her clothes and ran out the room. Halfway down the street, she realized she had left the camera in her hotel. Damn, she couldn't go back now.

Ronald hopped out of the car and flourished open the door. "For you, madam," he said and lowered his voice, "God, you look sexy."

Quickly, she checked the buttons on her blouse. OK. She failed to see the seductiveness of her faded jeans, especially since she packed into them like so much bulk cream cheese. Nodding good humoredly, she slid in next to Andre who was driving.

"This land," said Ronald, "is sort of primal to me. My mother was born somewhere here along the coast."

"This coast," said Andre, "reminds me of California. Have you ever been to Point Lobos?"

"Yes," said Susan.

"Were you ever in UFW work?" asked Colin.

"The most I ever did was picket the Safeway. And of course I haven't eaten a grape in seven years."

"I can see you're a very determined lady," said Andre.

She smiled, patiently waiting for the rest of the comment. She resented, as always, the effort required to cover up someone else's inanity. But that was all he had to say. They both tuned into the radio.

"*The Last Thing on My Mind*—it's the best thing that Judy Collins does," said Andre.

"Judy Collins is some woman," added Ronald. "Did you read her discussion of bisexuality in *Rolling Stone*?"

"No," admitted Susan.

"Say, what do you think of lesbian relationships?" asked Colin. "I mean the kind that women get into for political reasons. Do you think that the separatists are in the vanguard of the Women's Movement?"

"Oh, come on now," frowned Ronald. "Surely it has to be a mutual thing, the struggle against sexism. Chauvinism keeps down men too. It means we can't express our emotions. It means women can't seduce us. We're all constrained by sexist socialization."

"Don't you think . . ." she started.

"But I say radical lesbianism gives women the headstart that they need," said Andre. "You have to remember their handicaps from years of oppression."

" 'Handicaps' is a rather unfortunate word . . ." Susan began.

"I'm not saying women haven't been royally fucked over," said Ronald. "I'm not saying they haven't been screwed more than us."

She turned back to the landscape. It *was* like California— except that it was out of proportion. Everything looked so diminutive in comparison to North America. The contours were smaller; the colors faded. Sometimes travelling in Britain seemed artificial, inconsequential, like making love with the wrong person. She wondered if her consciousness had been shaped irrevocably by American land. In the same way, she could never enjoy Tennyson after reading Whitman. Maybe she had O.D.'d on American dimension.

"Do you see that?" asked Ronald. "The Last Inn. This is the furthest west in Britain, the closest we can get to home."

The men drank several pints of West Country cider. Susan had half a pint. Although she felt a slight feminist imperative to drink as much as the men. The more they drank, the keener they became about climbing. Ronald, especially, looked like he had already gone over the edge. It was almost 12:30.

"I'm ready when you chaps are," said Andre. "Pardon, when you *people* are."

Susan and Colin struck on ahead of the others. "What do you do for a living?" he asked her.

"Documentary journalism," she said.

"Have you ever published anything?" asked Ronald who was just catching up with them.

"Yes, I make my living from free-lance work."

"That must give you lots of free time to come on holidays like this," said Andre agreeably.

"I'm here in Cornwall to do some preliminary work on a book about Celtic independence movements."

Andre nodded. "I know what you mean. A photographer— or a writer—needs the autonomy of his own project."

"Do you write, too, Andre?" she asked politely.

"I do a bit of reviewing for the *Times,* for a little money. Actually, I'm preparing my own book of criticism."

Colin was a community worker in Glasgow. Something called a local catalyst.

Ronald told her about his three-year law career in Evanston, Illinois, which he had left six months before in order to get his head together. Everything he owned was in a rucksack in the car.

"Our marriage was the classic American split-up," Ronald said. "I really grew away from her when I went to law school. I feel tremendously guilty about it because she supported me."

Andre and Colin had dropped behind, arguing about their Gestalt leader. She listened to Ronald.

"Then I became close to one of the other law students," Ronald continued. "I tried to maintain an open relationship with Marie, my wife, but she was too traditional. She didn't realize our love was strained by the exclusivity. In short, I couldn't live without a dimension of passion."

Susan didn't see that she was walking too fast until he said, "Well, I guess I'm holding you back. You obviously take better care of your body."

"You two, hang about," shouted Andre.

They were a quartet again with their silly songs and bad puns.

Susan said she wanted to push on faster. Ronald accused her of being the all-American consumer, more concerned with quantity than quality, with miles than with . . . . She didn't catch the last part. Andre wanted to recollect in tranquility. So they all agreed to meet at the Miner's Arms pub in St. Just.

Colin also seemed relieved to be released from the others. He explained how the weekend had made him question his politics. "I mean, what does organizing a kids' hockey team have to do with Scottish nationalism? My job is pretty reform-ist. Ronald pointed this out. He sees the holes in things very clearly."

"What else does he see?"

They smiled to each other and moved along in easy silence.

The Miner's Arms was crowded. Old men leaned as close to the bar as their stomachs would allow and watched the young-er men play darts. A shame to miss these fine shots, she thought. Too highly-rouged ladies sat at the wall, sipping Guinness and chatting. A pampered black poodle snuggled between them. Susan and Colin devoured four rounds of cheese and tomato sandwiches in ten minutes. As Colin went to the bar for more, she luxuriated in the gregariousness of the pub. Such a release from the intensity of Andre and Ronald. It wasn't until 2:30 that she started to worry.

If they were going to get back before dark, they would have to leave within twenty minutes. Why couldn't those guys show a little consideration? She supposed they could always take the bus back to Penzance. Not to worry. They would find their own way out. She finished the rest of her beer with deliberate slowness. By three o'clock she was less determined.

"Say, what do you think has happened to those guys?" she roused Colin.

"Right, oh Chrike, I didn't even look. They should have been here a half-hour ago. They've probably fallen off a cliff or something."

"Don't even say that," she answered crossly.

"Well, maybe we should go and find them before they do fall off."

They walked briskly through the misty afternoon. It wasn't raining, not vertically. Wet wind swept through their parkas. She wondered why the light was so different here in England. And she could never get used to the early winter dark.

"Don't look so worried," he said. "We'll find them."

"I wasn't worried," she lied. "They should be easy to spot." She tried to lighten her voice. "Andre had on that ugly sheepskin jacket and Ronald had the red parka."

"Right," he walked on ahead of her, peering through the fog at the hills.

"They took a half-hour to climb that first stretch," she said. "They should be here by now."

The cliffs were quickly submerging into greyness, no red or white buoys.

"Slower than we thought," said Colin. "Maybe Andre used up all his energy talking. Or maybe Ronald paused to fuck a sheep along the way, to get in touch with his fellow creatures." He was silent for several minutes and then turned back to her in desperate anger. "Where *the hell* have they gone?"

Drizzle shredded the mist. It felt like they were walking through a wet net. She was chilled, exhausted, petrified. She blamed the romantic imagination which brought her here in the first place. OK, so she had wanted Arthurian terrain. She had wanted distant, sunny vistas of crumbling castles. What she got was a cold, damp hike searching for refugees from the twentieth century.

Putting his arm around her shoulder, Colin said, "Don't look so worried. We'll find them."

"You said that ten minutes ago. Don't *you* get uptight." She stopped abruptly. "Hey, aren't these familiar?" She picked up some orange worry beads from the sand.

"Oh, god, they're Ronald's," he said. "His favorite obsession. Oh, god."

"Hey, hey, calm down Dr. Watson. We don't have a corpse yet. Let's go back a bit. We must have walked past them."

The hard, yellow street lights of St. Just glared from the emptiness like distant sulphur torches lit by absent citizens. The footpath toward the town was barely discernible. The cows in the nearby field had blurred into twilight. A lone sheep moved over the rocks down by the waves. "Hey, isn't that them?" she asked. "Isn't that Andre's coat?"

Colin loped down the hill, ignoring the path, shouting, "Where the fuck have you guys been?"

When she caught up, Andre and Colin were standing with their hands on their hips looking down. "Insane. Insane," Andre was saying. "It's my fault. Insane. Insane."

Susan looked at him closely, as if fixing him in her stare would steady him. "Where is Ronald?" she asked slowly.

"In the cave. In the cave. Down there, can't you see?"

No, she couldn't see. She couldn't see anything. Night on the cliffs. A trial for true knights. "How long has he been there?" she asked. "Is he all right?"

"I was telling him about *The Manticore* by Robertson Davies."

"Andre," she shouted, "Is Ronald all right?"

"I don't know. I don't know." He turned toward the ocean and flapped his arms. "He just hasn't come out."

She knelt down and peered into the dark cave, calling, "Ronald. Ronald."

A noise surfaced. A long, low noise. She couldn't tell if it was the wind or the sea or a moan. She couldn't hear below Andre's wailing. "Colin, will you try to calm him down?"

"Ronald. Ronald," she shouted.

Again. A peculiar, childlike sound. Fearful, pathetic, desperate. A faint, wordless cry.

"OK, Ronald," she called. "Get ahold of yourself. We're here. Hold on."

She turned her head back toward Andre. "How deep is it? Why can't he get out?"

"He told me he was all right," said Andre. "I had read about it in this book. Always hoped to find one. A cave, I mean. In the book, a man goes through the cave and finds himself in the process of coming out. Ronald said he would go first and I would follow. About a half-hour ago. He got caught."

She interrupted Andre, trying to draw out a clearer story. But he continued as before. "It was my fault. My idea. He got caught on a rock or something. Maybe the tide frightened him. Couldn't move either way. It's the water. The water. The time. I know I should have left to get help. But I was . . . paralyzed. Afraid I would never find him again. I thought you would come." His voice broke and he began weeping. "I waited forever."

"Now hold on," she said, "it's not your fault. It's not our fault. Look, what are we drivelling on about? There's a man down there who's going to drown in high tide if we don't do something."

Susan measured the width of the cave. "It's a problem of time. That tide probably has a half-hour. Maybe we could get help from the village if we ran. Maybe not."

"What can we do?" shouted Andre.

"Colin, why don't you get up to St. Just?" she said. "You run. I'll try to do what I can here. I'll try to release the rock or whatever's catching him."

"No, no. I'll do it." Colin moved her to the side and peered into the cave. "I'm stronger."

"It's the only way," she said. "I'm the only one who's small enough. Please," she shouted. "We don't have time."

He ran off toward the yellowed village.

"Ronald," she shouted. "Listen, Ronald. We're coming down to get you." She heard the moan again. "Try to prop yourself up as high as you can. I know you're tired, Ronald, but try."

Andre was standing over her, tapping his walking stick against the opening. "He said he didn't know who he was, bound up by all those pressures," Andre spoke frantically. "I told him he was being rash, impatient."

Why couldn't he shut up for a minute? Susan was sorry for Andre, but she was more worried about Ronald. And if she told him to be quiet, he would just start sobbing again. Suddenly she said, "Andre, the stick. Have you got any matches?"

"I smoked my last cigarette twenty minutes ago, sorry."

"I don't want a cigarette," she snapped. "Do you have any matches, Andre? Quick."

"Matches. Yes, here, but . . . ."

"And the stick."

He looked at her blankly.

"The walking stick." She pulled it out of his loose grip. "It's the only piece of dry wood around here."

Before he could protest, she was trying to ignite the cane.

"Have you gone mad?" shouted Andre. "Take hold of yourself, Susan. What are you doing?" He tried to wrestle the cane from her.

"Light. Don't you see? Light. To look inside the cave. To get a sense of dimension. To see how Ronald is." She spit out the words, more and more anxious about the stick. Finally it caught the flame. Backing away from the glare for a moment, she thrust it firmly into the black hole. She could see the moist, jagged ridges of the cave, then the edge of its crouched inhabitant. All she could recognize was Ronald's back. A patch of red parka. The flame went out.

"Ronald. Ronald. Can you hear me, Ronald?" Another low moan rose. The contortion of his body must be terribly painful. How could he have done it? How could they get him out? Why was he doubled over? He must have changed his

mind about how to get out. He must have turned upside
down and tried to swim out the bottom. But the cave was too
narrow to exit there. So now he was stuck, with his head and
feet facing down. His back wedged across the cave. Caught
both ways. Worse than she thought. She had counted on his
height giving them time against the tide. But he lost three feet
by bending over. Ten minutes? Maybe fifteen. Colin would
never make it back.

A faint sound surfaced.

"How is he?" Andre demanded.

"See for yourself." She lit the cane and turned toward the
village.

"No. I'm a coward," said Andre. "I admit it. Just tell me
how he is. Does it look hopeful?"

"No." She looked over the ocean now, the cane flaming in
her hand. It left her blind against the black water, as if she
were using flashbulbs in a long, dark tunnel.

"Why?" said Andre.

"He's got himself stuck in a Chinese puzzle. Caught both
ways."

"Poor Ronald. He was so afraid of something."

She stamped out the flame and removed her parka.

"What are you doing?" he asked.

"I'm going down."

"Without the flare?"

"It wouldn't do any good," she said, lowering her foot
carefully. "It's a matter of feeling out the wedges, of grabbing
and holding. Anyway, there's no room for it."

"You're crazy," he screamed. "At least wait until they get
back."

"There's nothing to wait for, or there won't be," she got a
foothold. "He'll be gone by that time, if he's not already."

"Well, what are you going to do?"

"I don't know."

◇

She placed one foot close after the other, climbing deeper. Deeper. Her left foot slipped and she could feel the shoe loosen. She heard it swoosh off her foot. It seemed to take minutes before it landed on Ronald's back. A thud, followed by a groan. At least he's alive, she thought and cried, "Oh."

"Are you OK?" shouted Andre. He hadn't needed to shout. She was just an inch or two below the beginning.

"Yes. Don't worry about me yet. Think about ropes— things we can use to pull us out. Your belt. And that strap from Ronald's handbag."

"And my binoculars," he shouted.

"Right." The waves were higher than she anticipated. Her only chance was to dislodge Ronald, attach him to a rope and pull him up after she climbed out.

Her foot slipped and the rock on which she was balancing crumbled against the wall. She thought she would fall straight on Ronald. Her only reaction was acceptance. A sense of inevitability. No regret or fear. No reaction, really. But she felt a ledge below and managed to catch herself diagonally across the tunnel.

"Are you all right?" shouted Andre.

"Yes," she said, "yes." His panic was oddly reassuring. It gave her something to react against. Steadied her. She felt a cold chill run down one leg, paralyzing her for a second. Then another chill. It was the water. The waves spitting. The water. Everything accelerated. She felt like the film had snapped and the projector was speeding. Dark. Water. Hard, rock edges. Cold. Roars from the waves; echoes from the cave. Sloshing feet inside and outside. Moans from Ronald. "Are you all right? Are you all right?" She realized she was the one who was supposed to answer. She felt free. A sense of release. Surrender would be so easy. No one to see or hear. No one else. She caught herself. She groped for Ronald with her foot. He was just beneath her. She could feel his warmth through the parka. She could also feel the wet.

The tide had risen. Water just below her feet now. And above her were sheer walls, the ones she had fallen past.

Straddled over him, her legs astride the tunnel, she bent down to pull him up. Frantically, purposely, systematically, she tried various ways of releasing him. He couldn't budge. Impossible. One life, feelings fragmented her thoughts. One death, one life, were enough.

"Are you all right? Are you all right?" She wished she could reassure Andre. She slipped down to something soft.

"No," she shouted suddenly. She ranged her hands over the sides of the cave. No way to climb back up. Water had reached her ankles. Standing on tiptoes, she was revolted that her support was Ronald's back. She could feel the slipperiness of his parka through her stocking. Something. One finger touched something. Some kind of projection above her head. Not tall enough, she was not tall enough and the water . . . the water was reaching her knees. She felt a sudden anxiety about her watch. The watch she had bought in Switzerland years ago. The watch wasn't waterproofed. She pulled the chain over her head and swung it, lasso-like, in the direction of the protrusion just above her head. It caught and held steady. Very precisely and forcefully she tugged it. Working as a lever, it supported her to the ridge several inches above. Surprised by the endurance of the chain, she felt a twinge of remorse as the watch smashed against the wall of the cave. What was that John Cameron Swayze commercial with all the water rising faster and faster and . . . .

"Are you all right?"

"Yes," she said. "Yes." On her way out now, no question. As the water lapped after her, she strained and pushed and forced her way out. The momentum was there. The water was more reminder than threat. She knew she would make it. That was certain. And for the last minute of straining and stretching, she actually enjoyed this sensation of movement. She caught sight of a fire at the top of the cave. Torches. They lit the faces of four men. Four serious, worried—and now—relieved faces.

"Ronald?" asked Colin. "We've lost him?"

"Yes," she said.

72

"But you're all right?" asked Andre. You're all right?"
She nodded.

◊

Susan was sitting alone, sorting through a dozen contact
sheets. The village shots were OK, but she would have to go
back with a filter for the cliff photographs. It was odd to be
back in Cornwall after all these months. She was glad she had
returned for the inquest.

◊

The hearing was brief and uneventful. Ronald's wife had re-
quested the body. The cave had been sealed off by the Council. Testimony was finished in an hour. This inquest reminded Susan that her sadness for Ronald had not ended, would
probably never end. It revived old fears and she was grateful
to realize that some of these *had* already ended. The memory
of that afternoon was like a cold fog through which her heart
passed during splinters of her nightmares and during twinges
in uneasy days. But she knew she would be OK. For her the
inquest was a sober commencement ceremony. She knew she
would be OK.

After the hearing she climbed into the familiar old car with
Andre and Colin. They exchanged news. Both men were surprised her book was almost finished. Andre said his life was
going well. He was coming to terms with his ambition. Working full time to pay for his psychoanalysis. Going every day
helped him a lot. Colin barely got a word in. He said he was
standing as a Scottish National Party candidate. The inquest
was making a big dent in his campaign, still he had wanted to
come down for it.

Colin offered her a lift North. Andre invited her to have
lunch. But she said she had more photographs to take. So
they both promised to write and dropped her off at the beach
alone.

Cultured Green

Hot, crowded, chickens underfoot. Suffocating, but if she opened the window, the pig on the roof might piss in her face again. Mother had told her those Towel Moists would come in handy. So what was a nice Job's Daughter, *magna cum laude* social studies teacher from Seattle doing in a twenty-year old Bluebird school bus sputtering from Guatemala City to Oaxaca on the grace of a reconditioned rear axle and a dust-streaked statue of the Blessed Virgin?

Six months from Southern Chile. Buses all the same vintage, all with the same Noah's Ark contingent. Six months of brown-bellied Australians who drove vans cushioned with semen-caked sleeping bags. She was ready to go home. She didn't know if she belonged in the States. She did know she didn't belong here. Rudolfo's wild orchid was dying from its own steam in the plastic bag at her feet. Her backpack was stuffed with mementos from Eduardo in Santiago, Anna in Rosario, Señora Pardo in Belem. Remarkable hospitality. Volcanoes of food. The best bed in the house. Nothing accepted in return. One thing, expected, in return. If it were not too much trouble (the best English, including the subjunctive, in cases like this), did she know a school for their brother Juan or Lupe or Raul? Her new friends—they were the innocents abroad. This responsibility they gave her was heavy and maybe that's why she was going home. The further north she went, the hotter it got. The orchid was dead an hour ago.

Too hot to read. Too hot to write. Too hot to eat. Not that she had much. Fifty dollars to the border and a plane ticket from there. A box of Arrowroot cookies, a can of Spam, a loaf of bread she bought yesterday in Guatemala City. The cookies were all she had last night. Still, she couldn't bear to open the can of carnal imitation. Maybe she would chew on the bread. Maybe that would wake her from this goddamned stupor.

The Indian woman in the next seat watched closely, more fascinated by the khaki youth hostel backpack than by its contents. The woman was from Nabaj. You could tell by the *huipuil*. What was she doing this far north? After six months, you get used to observing and being observed.

The bread was moldy. Green pimples. Since yesterday? Had they cheated her? Did they know it was rotten? Gringa sucker. How could she get mad at them? She had fifty dollars to get to the border. Fifty dollars was gold to them. Cortez stole the gold from Montezuma. She closed her eyes. She would be home soon. Whatever that meant. And now they were pulling into La Puerta. There was bound to be at least some warm Coke at La Puerta.

She took only her wallet and the bag of bread with her when she got off the bus. Once she bought the Coke, she chugged it greedily, and walked toward a fence where she could dump the loaf of bread. As she moved the bread over the edge of the fence, she felt a tug, pulling back her hand. The woman from Nabaj. She looked at the Indian woman silently and released the bag. The woman, whose face shone with determined indifference, put the bread under her *huipuil* and returned to the bus. It was 4:15, July 20, six months on the road.

VII

Cooperative

Susan had a terrible time finding the cooperative. They
told her to look for the broken-down factory on Hemingford Road, but she cycled by the New You Bra Company
three times before recognizing the building. As Susan chained
her bicycle to the wrought iron gate, a sari floated past her.
Odd to think of herself and this Indian woman both as immigrants. They had moved to such different Englands.

Inside, the building was colder than outside, drafty. A
heavy metal door resisted the latch. Wind lashed down
through broken windows. Susan stepped around the clutter
of old furniture on the first landing. The corridor was littered
with cardboard boxes, rusting dollies, a dress rack with Santa
Claus costumes. She recognized this as the conscious neglect
with which people design their "alternative spaces." She almost missed the green sign, "Cooperative Press." Drafty even
up here. Securing the peacoat with its only remaining brass
button, she commended herself for appropriate dress.

The corridor turned into an open door—rather into an open
wall. Three people sat clustered at one end of the long factory
room, around a small electric fire. They were two pale women
and a thin, blond man.

The man looked up, waved with great angularity, strode
over to her and in a bright Australian accent, declared, "Hello,
you must be Susan."

Susan, who was staring at the women huddled over their
work, nodded.

"You're the girl Alexander sent, right?" He reached behind himself for the ringing telephone. "Hang on a minute. Hello, Gordon Moore speaking."

The cold red concrete floor was scattered with throw rugs in a desperate claim on warmth. And books. Parcels of books. Great 100 volume cases. The mailing table was piled with small packages. Galleys were draped over a sawhorse. Manuscripts, mostly unopened, spewed over a cluttered desk. Susan's Copperfield fantasies were interrupted by the bright posters: Madame Binh, Ché, Malcolm X, Leila Kahled, Chairman Mao and a blazing Soviet headline dated 1917. Shivering, she wished she had sewn on the other buttons, wished they owned more than one electric fire. The only warmth was an electric breathing from the New You Bra Company upstairs, a loud machine hum sewing through the ceiling. She wondered why the Indian woman had left so early. Had she been fired?

"Hey, Ghilly, Lynda. This is Susan, the journalist Alexander sent to solve all our problems."

Ghilly glanced up from her ledger and smiled. Lynda regarded Ghilly closely and said, "Welcome, we could use a Joan of Arc." Her voice was broad Yorkshire.

"Here, here." Gordon said. "Won't you have a cup of coffee? And let me show you around."

Reassured by scraps of paper on the floor, Susan thought of the frantic, busy, good days when she worked at *The Artisan.*

"That's the darkroom." he said. "Well, today it's the loo, but tomorrow with a little imagination, it's the darkroom." He plugged in the kettle.

Susan turned to laughter coming from the entrance. From a tall, red-haired woman and a friendly couple with a baby.

"Wina, Malcolm, Rita," Gordon shouted down the long room. "What's this? On time for a meeting? And just in time. I've plugged in the kettle and Susan had arrived to save us."

Susan sat in a corner of the couch sipping Sainsbury's instant coffee and watching them greet each other. Hugs, jokes, gossip. Running out to the shop for more long-life milk; moving the fire; boarding up a hole in the window.

"Rocks," sighed Gordon. "Damn kids. Come the revolution, they'll understand we're on their side."

Everyone laughed. They were friendly.

"Can you type?" Lynda asked.

"A little," Susan answered, trying to hide her disappointment and look cooperative.

"We all share the shitwork around here," Gordon explained.

"And the glory," laughed Malcolm.

"Ah, yes, the glory," sighed Wina.

Gordon cleared his throat. "Let's get down to business. How's the anarchist book, Wina?"

"Super," said Wina, her rich Dutch accent surfacing even in one word. "Just got ten more pages. Jan's lawyers smuggled them out. Not having so much luck with the women's stuff. Apparently security on them is tighter. I think if we could just postpone the printing two months, we'd have it."

Ghilly held her arms across her chest and spoke in a small, tight voice. "But we agreed to keep to timetable. Labor costs are going up in November. To say nothing of paper costs which have skyrocketed in the last year. We all *agreed* to stick to schedule."

"Come on, now, Ghilly," Wina leaned toward the smaller woman. "The Dutch government is going to cooperate with us as much as our anarchists cooperate with them. Nobody else would dare take on the politics of the book. We've got to do it, even if we're worried about losing a few quid."

"We're worried," said Ghilly sharply, "about losing the Cooperative if this goes on."

Susan was thinking of the book on Zimbabwe by her friend Alexander. "Too hot for the straight presses," he had said in an idiom that was 40 years younger than his own. If they were doing Alexander's book, Susan told herself, they were good people, good political people.

"On the bright side," said Rita, "I sold forty-five *Chile Diaries* to Queen Mary College."

"And I've rented a storefront on Camden Road for the women's bookshop," Gordon smiled.

"You what?" asked Ghilly.

"I think it's a fine idea," said Wina.

"It's now or not at all," said Gordon confidently. "I had to use a little entrepreneurial spirit."

" 'Gall,' I'd say 'gall.' " Ghilly shouted. "We're supposed to discuss that kind of decision. This is a cooperative, Gordon."

"Relax, love," he brought over another pot of instant coffee. "The city needs a women's bookshop."

Susan had first heard about the Cooperative from Alexander, during one of their lunches at Moishe's in Leicester Square. They used to meet there every week before his bout with pneumonia. At the beginning, they talked about Salisbury where she had spent two weeks and where he had lived for thirty years before his exile/escape to London. The intensity of their friendship came from those ineffable characteristics which cause expatriates to choose a common home, arriving at the same café from forty years and ten thousand miles apart.

"This Cooperative may be idealistic enough even for you," Alexander had teased her. "It may be enough to shake you out of this London drear."

"A situational depression," her therapist called it. Situation: she had a cold all winter from her freezing basement room. Situation: she had gained twenty pounds on lentils and white bread and not a little beer. Situation: her gas fire leaked. Sometimes she had visions of her grandfather who died of tuberculosis in Edinburgh. Sometimes she had dreams of Sylvia who drowned in gas two miles away in Hampstead. Situation: she didn't have any money. The average free-lancer in London made less than 2500 pounds a year. So she would opt for 15 pounds a week at a cooperative in a drafty warehouse? "Temporary insanity," her friend Carol would call it.

How like Alexander to worry about her. To forget about

his pneumonia and loneliness to tend to her sad face.

"Just what you wanted," Alexander had said. "Good politics. Good writing. I've reviewed one of their non-racist, non-sexist texts. They edit, publish and distribute themselves. You could write that book . . ." he interrupted himself. "The only problem . . . ."

"Is that there's no money," she said.

"How did you guess?"

But he explained that it would give her a base. And he was right, she needed to spend more time with people serious about publishing. Free-lance journalism was like a cottage industry. Susan fancied herself an old woman knitting all day in a Caithness croft and sending her wares to London. She hated the isolation. Deadlines and checks were her only link with the real world. The checks were infrequent and late. She would stand in the darkroom for hours, staring at the red light in passive resistance. If she finished this assignment, there would only be another. This was definitely not the London she had imagined. Maybe she would find it at the Cooperative.

◊

"How can a man run a women's bookshop?" Lynda was asking.

"I wouldn't run it, exactly," said Gordon defensively. "I just found us the space."

"And rented it already," reminded Ghilly.

Susan had hoped they would ask her some questions, tell her a little about what they wanted her to do, but it was getting late and Rita had to take the baby home for his nap. She would ask what happened to Alexander's book at the next meeting.

◊

The following morning Susan found Lynda alone typing labels and she joined in. Eight-thirty, "American Time" to start work. She could never get used to starting at ten o'clock the way they did here. Half the day seemed gone by then. Her British friends found such diligent Americanism to be quaint, rather schoolgirlish. She found their two hour lunches on Fleet Street romantically decadent at first and then plain boring.

When Ghilly and Gordon arrived, they seemed relieved to see Susan.

"Hey, man, good to see you," said Gordon. "Typing labels? Into the hard stuff already? Hey listen, we'll get that darkroom set up today or tomorrow."

Ghilly set in to washing yesterday's coffee cups. "Gordon," she said. "Look at the time, love."

"Right," he said. "Catch you later. I've got to get down to the Whitehall Gallery. They're interested in Malcolm's prints."

Lynda looked up from her labels. "Why didn't you bring that up at the meeting yesterday?"

"I thought everybody knew," Gordon said briskly. "Look, I'll give you the details soon as I return. Can anybody take care of unpacking those IRA books while I'm downtown?"

Ghilly told Susan that she and Gordon had been editing until 11:00 p.m. the previous night. She was worried about Gordon's ulcer. No matter how much they all shared the work, no matter how many workers they took on, Gordon was frenetic. Some people had problems with inertia. Gordon suffered from centrifugal force.

Susan liked Ghilly. One of those *very sensible* Englishwomen. Oxbridge without the tailored drawl and dress. Her modesty came from integrity rather than inhibition. Ghilly was absolutely the sort you would expect to wind up with an unschooled political refugee from Brisbane. She had no doubts about her right to change the world.

"I'll stack the books," said Lynda.

That left Susan the rest of the labels. She didn't mind the tedium; she was just glad to have something of her own to do.

The rape book arrived that week. A month late, so they skipped their meeting. No time for lunch or even coffee as they hustled books off to the shops. Susan piled a dozen copies in her basket and cycled down to the Women's Liberation Workshop in Soho. Such a crisp May day. The black taxis gleamed like beetles after a rain. While she waited for the light to change at Tavistock Square, Susan watched a Japanese couple in matching Fairisle sweaters rushing off to pay tribute at the statue of Ghandi. The woman carried a huge Selfridge's bag. Coasting through the traffic, not one bus farted in her face. Susan felt something she hadn't felt in months—that she was in London, not in some dreary, damp, tense shadow of a city, but that she was in London and there were reasons to be here.

◇

At the Coop meeting that Friday, which was kept short because they still had 300 rape books to deliver, Susan asked when they were scheduling Alexander Norton's book.

Everyone except Gordon looked blank.

"The Zimbabwe poet?" asked Rita. "But he's under contract to Longman's."

"They don't want the new book," Susan explained. "They say he's lost his edge."

"More likely his edge is too sharp for their liberal politics," said Gordon. "I told him we would probably do the book."

"But," Susan stumbled. "He thinks it's definite."

"He's in his seventies," said Rita blankly, "and not very well, I understand."

"Of course, let's see the book," said Ghilly.

They liked Susan's suggestions for illustrating the Dutch anarchist material. And although Ghilly was apprehensive about costs, they told Susan to start shooting next week.

◇

On Monday, Gordon arrived alone, looking tired and tense. "Ghilly has bronchitis again. She got it last year too. Oh, hell, what a time, man. She was supposed to go up to Leeds peddling books tomorrow. It's these damn broken windows. Damn, drafty room. Impossible to heat. Damn London weather. Dampness everywhere. It took a month to get those appointments in Leeds. Poor Ghilly. We had to wait two hours at the Health Collective last night. Damn Leeds."

Susan moved a manila envelope over her picture layouts, so Gordon wouldn't see them. "She'll be OK with a little rest. It's warm at your flat, isn't it?"

He nodded distractedly.

"And I'll go up to Leeds for you."

He smiled, "For us, man."

"I can leave tomorrow morning."

"But you won't know what you're doing. You've never done it before. You don't know about discounts and delivery dates and PR on the new books."

"I've got a whole day to learn."

"Half a day. You really should take the five o'clock coach from Victoria tonight to make those morning appointments."

◇

When Susan got to Leeds, half the appointments fell through.

"A month ago?"

"Cooperative what?"

"Sorry, no time; the Penguin man is in town."

Maybe Gordon was right. Maybe she didn't know what she was doing. Her inexperience was a failure for the whole Cooperative.

"How do you cooperate?" Finally, a friendly voice.

He was a heavy old man, with the liberal streak you expected to find in a university bookstore.

Was he being snide? Susan wondered. Who cared? He was the only person who had asked her to sit down all day. Maybe she could sell a small order, through charm or pity.

"We all work together," she said, trying not to sound like a tired record. "We all share the soliciting, the editing, the dispatching, the publicity, the income. We all came to it with different skills."

"And yours is?"

"I'm a journalist. Photography and reporting. Right now I'm planning pictures for a book about Dutch politics."

"Which of these books is yours?" He seemed interested.

"Oh, none of them yet," she said. "I've only been there a few months."

He looked disappointed and then pensive. "I guess there's a lot of clerical work to do. It's always like that, isn't it?"

Susan was confused.

"Don't look so surprised. I worked on *Red Net* in the early days. Why do you think I took time to see you? I'll order six of each book—by consignment."

On the coach home, she sketched her shots and the design for the cover of Wina's book. It was late, after 9:00 p.m., by the time she got up to Hemingford Road. The downstairs door of the old factory was unlocked and Susan felt at once relieved. Someone would be there. Gordon. She wanted—needed—two things from him: reassurance that Leeds was a tough town and some enthusiasm for the Dutch photos. The concrete steps were unlit. It was late. She was in a derelict building on a forgotten street in a big city, she reminded herself. The fear evaporated as quickly as it came. She just couldn't feel as scared here as she did driving down East 14th Street in Oakland during the middle of the afternoon. She sensed some diplomatic immunity against violence in Britain. "Sense, I'll give you sense," Carol would say. But she had never felt threatened in London.

Black. The room was black except for the spotlight of a tensor lamp over Gordon's notebook. He was scribbling on a yellow pad between the calculator and the ledger. She couldn't see the orange glow of the fire filaments.

"It's freezing here," she said, reaching down to switch on the fire. She stopped, noticing that Gordon was wearing his RAF coat. "What's this? An economy move?"

Susan wanted to make a joke about Australian radicals wearing colonial military attire, but Gordon immediately began to complain about the printer's invoice, about how no one was around to help him.

"Rita is off academicing at some language conference. Malcolm, as always, is absorbed in his prints. Wina's lover from Amsterdam is here. I've got no idea how all the IRA books are going to be distributed."

Susan said she would help—after she set up the darkroom.

"The darkroom," Gordon exploded. "Everybody's in this for himself. With Wina, it's for her anarchist friends. With Malcolm, it's for his prints."

"But you're the one who's always talking about artists having respect for themselves as workers."

"Personally," said Gordon, "I think survival comes before the privilege of self-respect. Somebody has to do the shit-work."

Susan's voice was lost somewhere between disappointment and anger. She walked silently toward the corridor. "OK," she said finally, patiently, reminding herself again that revolutions take time. "I'll be here at 8:30 tomorrow to help distribute the books. But let's talk about shit and privilege at the next Coop meeting."

◇

Alexander's book was at the printers. Everyone was excited about it. Gordon explained to the meeting that the Zimbabwe book would make the Coop connections in the black community. The print run would be ten thousand. Large for the Coop, but, of course, far below what Alexander was used to with Longman's.

"Alexander understands our bind," said Gordon.

It should have been a cheerful meeting, but everyone was strained and tired. Lynda worried about Gordon's unilateral decision to open a woman's bookshop.

"Unilateral decision," Gordon repeated angrily. "How about unilateral work! I'll be happy to share the decisions— and the work."

Rita interrupted. "Look, Gordon, we've been through this before, haven't we? We all have other jobs. I've got Malcolm and the baby to support. It was your choice to spend twenty hours a day here."

"And what if I didn't?" he shouted.

Wina leaned forward. Susan was fascinated by Wina: the

pink "Frau-Offensive" t-shirt with the Vent Vert perfume and the declassé roach clip around her neck.

"I think we're geting emotional," Wina cleared her throat huskily. "It's not the decision, itself, Gordon. It's the way it was made. We agreed to consult on everything. Remember?"

"See if I care," he threw up his hands. "I'll go give back the lease now. Don't listen to me. You'll see." He pulled on his coat and strode away. "You'll see. London needs a women's bookshop."

◇

No one was wrong. That was the difficult part. Everyone had a right to be consulted. Together they had imagined the Cooperative, invested in it, worked for it. They should all be part of the decisions. However, they didn't have Gordon's dedication or centrifugal urgency.

Throughout the week, they held little caucuses about "the situation." Wina and Rita resolved to spend more time at the warehouse. Ghilly separately lobbied Malcolm for sympathy, patience or whatever his gentleness might mean. She came to Susan, too. Ghilly appealed to her as someone who spent so much time at the office, who must think Gordon's decisions were sound ones. Wina and Rita asked Susan if she didn't find Ghilly and Gordon a little paternalistic.

One night Susan stayed late with Gordon to mail off a press release. He told her about all the workers who had come and gone since the Coop's beginnings three years before.

"No one wants to slog," he said. "Teamwork. Look who stayed tonight. No one."

◇

"All one happy family," said Malcolm as he opened the Cooperative meeting the next week.

"Sit down, Gordon," Rita said gently. "You look exhausted."

"I am tired—damn tired—of sitting through rush hour traffic on that damn 17 bus."

"Stand, then," said Rita. "Look, I've been thinking about

the uneven distribution of work."

"And of the decision making," said Wina.

"Yes," Gordon answered quickly. "Very absorbing problems. But somewhat abstract and personal compared to the distribution of the *Chile Diaries,* our rent and the printing bill."

Wina leaned forward in a wave of Vent Vert. "May I remind you that the personal is political."

"The economic is more political," rasped Gordon, "if you remember a little of that dialectical materialism from your CP lover—or was he the one last week?"

"Let's not get personal," Malcolm laughed, alone.

◇

A reconstitution, they called it. A few compromises. "We don't live in an ideal world," Wina said, agreeing to postpone her book until they knew the profits from the *Diaries.* I'll try to keep the big decisions for weekly meeting," Gordon conceded. Rita admitted it would be practical for him to make a few emergency decisions by himself.

Susan left the Coop early that night, before the sulphur lights. Gordon had asked her what was wrong and she said she didn't know. She really didn't know why it was all falling apart around her. Without Wina's book, there would be no need for Susan's photographs. Not now. Not ever? Tonight she could see herself for who she was, a label licker and book packer in a cold London warehouse for 15 pounds a week. Her grandfather made 15 pounds a week and died of tuberculosis. "Temporary insanity." Carol was right. You can fool with reality, you can romanticize only so long. Then physical parameters like sickness and death intervene.

◇

They met again at Moishe's Cafe. Alexander asked her loving questions about the photography, her friends, the Cooperative. Susan answered briskly and was halfway through the humus before she could be honest.

"Someone isn't being cooperative," she said nervously. Then the tears and complaints and guilt flooded out.

"What's wrong with me?" she demanded. "Why do I believe in last peace marches and cooperative Cooperatives?"

Alexander held her in his tired, watchful eyes.

"Am I crazy? Are they hypocrites?" she asked. "No, they're good people. But it's so much more complex than I imagined. Having to survive. Having to work and deal with personal problems and edit and publish and distribute and keep a good political line. Am I too young?"

"Not *too* young," said Alexander.

"How can I go on?" The tears fell from shame and confusion. "Months have passed and they still don't want my photos. They're still arguing about the color of the labels. Gordon is still making unilateral decisions. It's not a cooperative; it's a one-man band. Maybe if we struggled . . . maybe . . . ."

"You have a choice," he said quietly.

"Choice," she repeated, surfacing to his voice.

"Choice about whether you want to hear the one-man band or make a harmony or go back to your own work for a while."

She stared at him, feeling the unshed tears drain down her throat.

"This isn't the last cooperative," he said.

She looked closer. Her anxiety abated for the moment. She noticed how weary he looked, run-down. This was her fault. She should have been taking care of Alexander. He lived in the coldest of Highgate flats and never quite learned to make a proper cup of tea.

"I bet you've run out of Vitamin C," she said. "I got a new supply from mother. See, I've brought you a bottle. Brother Alexander, methinks you've not been taking care of yourself."

"Do thank your gracious mother. But let's get back to the problem at hand. You have a choice about the Cooperative. What are you going to do?"

"It's not as easy as you think. I've dragged so many friends into this mess. Joan of Arc, I am, leading the troops—into a brick wall."

"It's easier than *you* think."

"I even got my dear Alexander involved."

"That started before you."

"But I pushed it. I got you to sign their contract."

"Longman's won't do the book," he said tiredly. "I can't flog it around at my age. Time has made my choice. Besides the galleys look fine. What have I got to lose?"

◇

Susan wanted to stay in London until Alexander's book was finished. But the bindery was on strike which meant a six week delay. If she was going to take that magazine assignment in Morocco, she would have to go now.

When she officially quit at the Monday meeting, Rita, Ghilly, Malcolm and Lynda nodded in various degrees of resignation. Wina sighed. "It must have been like this at the Paris Commune." Gordon was busy scratching her name off the schedule. "OK, OK, it's your choice."

◇

After returning from Morocco, Susan secluded herself in the darkroom for days. One afternoon, she emerged to check a reference in the British Museum reading room. As she cycled past Dillon's Bookshop, she noticed the green Cooperative Press logo. And Alexander's book.

The cover was silhouetted just as he wanted it. The book looked thicker than she had imagined. It was a tasteful display, with a photograph of Alexander and a short memorium. The entire display window was bordered in black.

Love/Love

Listen, kid. She was just gorgeous. Glamorous.
Nineteen thirties chic. A pin-up type. You'll say
I'm just a mortal, sexist man, but honest, she didn't
mind being told she was glamourous, for all her
liberated notions. Took care of herself. Had her
hair done every week at Yosh. And watched her
figure like—as the saying goes—like all the men did.
Heh. Heh. Maybe she wore too much mascara,
but it really accentuated those ebony eyes. Then
there was that red, Jean Harlow mouth—1930s,
honest-to-god. Her legs were made for stockings.
In the summer they were tan and bare and all the
more sexy.

She took care of her looks, all right. And everything else. She wasn't satisfied with just being a
nurse. So she worked her way up to Supervisor.
That bored her after six months. At thirty, with
a great career ahead, she applied for medical school.
She got in, with a scholarship, of course. A very
bright girl as well as sexy. Not that you were
allowed to dawdle over the latter. Like all good
catches, she was hooked four or five years ago. A
real super guy. Lots of money. Nice house. I
mean they had *everything* together.

But she got it into her pretty head, about the same time she decided to apply for med school, that she wanted out of the marriage. Not that I was disappointed, personally, to hear about it. But it did seem kind of rash. She had a life that wasn't all that bad, from the outside.

The whole story is like Richard Corey. Remember the Simon and Garfunkel song? Well, that's what happened, more or less. First, she changed her mind. Decided she couldn't bear to leave the lucky bastard. Then one night last week she drove over to the Nimitz and slammed her orange Volvo into a siding at eighty miles an hour. Smashed the whole car. Totaled. And broke every bone in her beautiful bod . . . well, she did get some pretty severe lacerations on that face. And worst of all, there's some kind of head damage. Maybe not permanent, but it'll take her a couple of years to regain control of her memory bank or whatever it's called. Luckily, she has her husband to take care of her. I don't get it. She was such a glamourous girl. Bright. Just gorgeous.

VIII

Other Voices

The dark room was stale with the smell of cupboards and drawers unused by one-night tourists. *Heavy. Hot. Only a minute ago she had shut out the wind, shut in the flying curtains. Only half a minute ago she had asked Mohammed to leave her. She would be all right alone. Alone. ALONE. She had bolted the door and now she was paying for her pride with a headache. Throbbing like banging. Bang, bang, banging, like someone knocking at the door. She ought to open it. She ought to. What if no one were there? What if, what if, what if this was all a dream. Decisions were endless. Where was the door? How could she open it? The top. Her fingers scratched the top. They were red. Blood red? Not nail polish red. She never wore nail polish. Pagan ritual, Sister Teresa, first grade. Sexist conditioning, Sister Morgan, graduate school. Nail polish was a mistake, like the red dress she wore that late night, lost in Gastown. The bottom of the door was closed too. But she could feel air at the bottom. Perhaps she should just lie there at the door's edge and breathe deeply. In and out. Ways out. There must be ways out. The same ways as in. Openings. Try the bolt. Try unlocking the bolt. The handle. Turning the handle. Turning.*

Turning over in the bed, Susan saw that the watch on the arm that wiped her brow said three o'clock. She moved in and out of the nausea, the delirium. Out long enough to see a moon through the polyester pink and purple flowers. To see Mohammed sitting next to the window, soothing her with his even breathing, his head bent down in sleep like a priest in meditation. *Meditating on our sins after the procession. It wasn't hard to keep up in the procession. Pious pace. Mind on other things. Unquestioned answers. Meditating on the sorrowful mysteries. She was on her third decade and Mohammed was only a boy. The boy's watch said three o'clock. Three o'clock. How? It was dark outside. School wasn't even dismissed yet. Oh, yes, this was the OTHER side of the world. And she was with the African man, no boy. In the dream a few minutes ago, they had gone through the earth. Susan had gone through the dark bowels with a boy. With her little brother. With her divorced husband. She had been walking along, holding hands with her son. She kept getting lost. She kept stopping to ask directions. And the boy began to cry. Because he wanted to be fed. "Can't cook tonight, dear, I have to work late." "Hush, child, we'll get some more formula." Formula. She had always been bad at formulas. "One divided by two equals one-half." A divorcée was half a person. "One plus one equals three," Father had written on the back of her fifty dollar wedding bill. "One from two equals one." At least her subtraction was always good.*

The boy was still asleep. Despite the wheels crocketing along behind the horses hooves three floors below. Despite the shuffling of sneakers in the hotel corridor. "Did you remember the water bottle?" "Shut up. People are trying to sleep in this place, you know." Despite the aroma of fresh coffee rising from the restaurant downstairs. Despite the sunrise heat pulling through the curtains. It had been crazy, the night, the day. How long had she been asleep? How long had this whole thing been going on? She would pull herself together. She would run it all through her mind, beginning at the beginning of the trip—in Agadir a week ago.

◇

"Putain!" shouted the two little girls in faded mini dresses. "Whore!" "Hure!" "Putain!" Susan knew she should just laugh at the absurdity of tourist language. Epithets would come easier with Esperanto. But something snapped. She was possessed by the Witch of the West, and she called back, "Pourquoi vous m'appelez comme ça? Pourquoi?" They raced up the stairs of their meringue white apartment building. She watched them running desperately from the madwoman, up to the seventh floor. She turned and walked toward the beach shops. She wasn't sure whether it was their resilience or her imagination which trailed after her. "Putain!" "Whore!" "Hure!"

Agadir was a mean, ugly city. Shabby mourning to an earthquake she watched on TV when she was nine years old. The late fifties concrete set the city as a cheap, hurried housing project. All the more grungy because it had been done in ridiculous white. At least Americans concealed their squalor in sooty brick shadows.

Garish orange and yellow caftans blew about the breezy doorways of the shops. Orange and red. Red and yellow. Appalling tourist gear.

"Madame, madame, donnez-moi un dirham."

"Bonjour, madame."

"Un dirham, madame."

Susan looked down into the brown eyes of a little boy and saw them looking back at this rich bitch from _____ ? No, that wasn't part of the game. He didn't care where she came from. She was an Englishgermanswede. A Westerner who spoke moneylanguage.

"No, No!" she heard herself shouting, one hand gripping a tinselly tourist dress for diplomatic sanctuary. "No, no!" she continued after he had run away. She needed to sit down somewhere and get hold of herself.

"Madame. Madame."

"No. No."

"Mais, madame."

It was a different voice. Older. One of those fucking Arab men.

"No, no!" she shouted. She released the dress and strode off past the gaping shopkeepers.

The voice stayed with her. "Madame." Persistent.

"Madame." Unwavering. "Madame."

Would he really do something in the middle of the city? In the middle of the day? With all these men watching? Why didn't somebody do something?

"Madame. Madame."

Probably more chance of getting raped in Berkeley, she had written to her mother, and the white slave trade was a racist myth. Susan neglected to mention that episode in Zanzibar a few years ago. But here in Agadir? It was just built in 1958, for godsake.

"Madame, s'il vous plâit."

Those were the last words she heard before falling down the steps. Talk about a klutz. It must be her period. She always felt like a giraffe during her period. She tried to summon Susie's judo lessons.

"Go *away*," she turned around with her witchiest expression to find a young man regarding her with amused concern.

"Please let me help you," he ventured toward her, one hand extended. She noticed he was speaking English and that his other hand held her Michelin Guide.

"You dropped it back in the stall, Miss."

She said thank you with mixed relief and resentment. Her Michelin Guide was a gift from her mother. If she had to go to such a primitive place, she might as well approach it sensibly.

"Are you all right?" he asked.

"Yes, thanks," she laughed, a sense of humor being the only grace left to her. "I'll be fine now. Good-bye and thanks again."

"Perhaps you should rest a minute."

"No, no. I'm OK, really." What did he think she was, some kind of old lady? A few minutes ago he was chasing after her nubile body and now he was playing Boy Scout.

"Won't you please join me for a mint tea? My uncle owns the Quatre Saisons," he pointed over to a cafe on the Avenue Kennedy, next to her pension.

"Uncle," sure, she thought. Just like the two kids who

wanted to show her around Fez were brothers, until they forgot each other's name.

"It's just Moroccan hospitality," he said. "Nothing else. I don't want to hassle you."

It was the "hassle" which touched her. He had studied English for six years at the lycée. He had won a scholarship to the Stanford University. Did she like mint tea? Because Uncle Ahmed also had Nescafé, Twinings, Coke, Fanta Orange.

She laughed easily. The kid was bright and sexy. Shadowy brown eyes, great curly hair and that broad smile. So much for culture and age. Age . . . *what* was she thinking about? She was ten years too late. But then again, maybe he had read about Graham Greene's aunt.

"More tea?"

"No thanks, Mohammed. I've got to get back to work, plan my itinerary, and write a letter."

"I'll be helping my uncle tomorrow morning," he said. "Maybe I'll see you here for breakfast? We have the best croissants on the Avenue."

◇

Grinning, she returned to the Hotel de France. The cool linoleum lobby was bare, except for three wooden chairs, some coverless copies of *Time* and *Woman's Own,* and the arborite table. The manager greeted her with the solicitude that had become obsequious as soon as they had stopped arguing about the twelve dirhams rent. The ubiquitous busboy-cum-taxidriver-cum-guide-of-Agadir also nodded, prepared to bring her anything from a martini to a Mohammed.

God, Mohammed was young. The same age as her little brother. Eighteen at most. This was the sort of movie that happened to middle-aged secretaries from Medicine Hat. She looked in the mottled mirror. The water stains made liverspots on her drawn face. She pulled her long, dark hair back into a rubberband. She could pass for . . . she could barely pass for twenty-nine which was what she was. That verticle line in her forehead was indelible now. She had started wearing these open-necked shirts because her bone structure was good. Oh, what the hell, Sophia Loren was forty-three and no one complained about her. But then Sophia Loren had Carlo Ponti and two kids. Susan's feminist guardian angel deserted her at night. Perhaps she should have stayed with Guy. Before the divorce, she had anticipated loneliness—a sort of Joni Mitchell melancholia—not the frantic pillow thrashing that she did, where the bed is too large and cold one minute, too hot and small the next.

A letter to Hilary. She could say anything to Hilary. Hilary had been the only one who agreed with her decision to travel alone.

"Why are the men so obnoxious?" she wrote. "Why can't I walk down the street without being touched up and talked at? I knew it was going to be a hassle, but this is *much* worse than Italy or Greece or even Mexico. They're like flies. I hear myself shouting, "Mouches, mouches." The worst part is that I find myself wishing I had someone—meaning some man—with me. So the independent lady journalist is chickening out after only seven days."

"Tangier, quel désastre. I suppose I expected to find Bob Dylan looking for the girl who left him behind. It was more like William Burroughs territory. Putrid pools and smashed bottles on the sidewalks. In a vacant lot across from my pension, kids chucked pieces of the demolished walls at each other. One night I was followed home by a guy with a knife and a lot of cultural pride which was wounded when I wouldn't buy his dope. Rabat and Casablanca were just as bad—too many tourists, but not enough to keep the mouches off my back. God, I sound like a raving racist."

A sign of age. Twenty-nine year old fascist. This week Susan had closed up to the people around her. What kind of conversation can you have with a guy who says, "Madame, I show you medina," or with the trendier adolescent card sharks who hang around the pensions? And the women? She had *no* communication with the women. It wasn't just that they didn't get to go to lycée and therefore didn't speak a Western language and didn't have contact with outsiders. It was those damn, impermeable veils behind which they giggled and gossiped and retreated.

She could always write anything to Hilary, anything without being judged. She couldn't admit the same defeats to Sally. She wrote Isadora Duncan journals to Sally—heady, gay, adventurous. Likewise, she understood that Sally's installments about the rich crust of Montreal's soirées anglaises were abridged versions of reality. They sent the letters to reassure each other; they wrote them to reassure themselves. A letter to Hilary, however, was a sort of marathon diary.

"I met a kid this afternoon. God, Mohammed *is* a kid. Still in lycée. Can I be that desperate, chasing after children? None of the men our age seem to qualify. They're all too sexist or too juvenile or too boring. Maybe those Y chromosomes really are retarded X's. Then I look at myself and I'm amazed that I have the nerve to be so choosy. It's OK now, while I've got a few good years left, but what's going to happen when I'm thirty-five or forty? I know this is terribly unfeminist of me to worry about, but my thighs are spreading; my spontaneity has withered; my feet are getting scaly. If I'm this much of a wreck now, what am I going to be like in six years? So although I don't want a man, I feel I have to find one while the picking is still moderate. I can't turn to women as lovers. I'm not saying that you made the wrong choice, but damnit, I want children."

Susan had had this same debate with Hilary many times in the last year—over coffee in Toronto, on the telephone after Hilary had moved off to live with Anita Evedaughter in Edmonton, and now airmail from Morocco. Susan was bored by her own preoccupation with "relationships." The word gave her a headache. She turned to her log book. Two more weeks of cultural anthropology. The research had seemed like a good idea last month: a subsidized trip to Morocco, a chance to test her new lenses. But tonight she could find no enthusiasm for the work. She stretched out, trying to fill the big bed. She consoled herself that she could leave Agadir in two days after the museum and a half roll of slides.

◇

"My Uncle Claude owns a hotel in Essaouira. Just the cure you need from the city," Mohammed said.

She knew something like this would follow the croissants and tea.

"No," she said halfheartedly, "I have to go further south, to the camel fair at Goulimime on Saturday."

"That's a big tourist show now. If you want to see the way Moroccans really live, you have to go to the coast. Essaouira is too windy for the German bus tours. No army bases either. Just Moroccans. People fishing, making things for the fishermen."

◇

As they fumbled to their bus seats at five the next morning, Susan got more than the usual stares. The young men were the most insinuating. One brushed against her breasts as she climbed into the next seat. The women didn't seem to giggle as much this morning. They gossiped behind their brown veils. Even the venerable old men—whose wizened faces would come out of her camera so beautifully if she could develop the guts to take close-ups—seemed to watch her. To watch the two of them. Customs officials could not guard unofficial customs. That was left to one's sense of propriety. ("Putain." "Whore." "Hure." "Putain.") Mohammed told her not to worry about them.

She took notes on the landscape for a while, increasingly distracted by the reckless lurches of the driver and the chickens pecking at the knapsack under her seat. She finally figured out the purpose of those rusty tin cans when a pregnant woman threw up in one and passed it on to her sister who did likewise. Susan handed them squares of the toilet tissue she always carried and some spearmint gum to wash away the taste. They accepted with hesitant gratitude. The procedure was repeated twenty minutes later: vomiting, tissue, chewing gum, wary exchange of glances.

Mohammed listened attentively as she confessed how frustrated she was trying to talk to Morrocan women. They seemed to be repelled by her, fascinated and threatened. She, herself, was never able to get beneath their layers of brown and grey polyester. Damn these robes—these habits—that even the brides of Christ at home had surrendered.

"They have their uses," he laughed. "It's easier to conduct an affair in my country. A woman can go visit a man as long as she likes. No one knows who goes in; who comes out."

("Putain." "Whore." "Hure." "Putain.")

She told him not to joke. None of the men in his country took women seriously. They either preyed or patronized. They were frightened and instead of hiding, themselves, they masked women in Arab chastity or Western wantoness. She caught herself and, in her best interviewer's tones, asked him what he thought.

He said he rarely had a chance to talk with Western women and if she didn't mind, he would prefer to listen right now.

Was he tame or cunning? She couldn't tell, but she admired his high cheekbones and his extraordinarily thick eyebrows.

("Dear, remember to be your sensible self." She heard her mother's voice. "All men suck." Hilary's voice. "Putain!" The girls in Agadir.)

"We're here," he said, regarding her with the scrutiny of one who is practiced at staring through veils. "This is Essaouira."

The 9:00 a.m. sun illumined a white village behind the ancient Portuguese scala. The tiled, turreted quiescence, was such a relief after Agadir. Gulls sailed lazily over the docks. Women, downed in layers of white, like plump doves, waddled across the sunny courtyards. Essaouira. The Hotel Tourisme was just over to the left. The little Arab boys who meet the buses in swarms gaped as Mohammed and Susan walked off together.

They were greeted by a grunt from an old woman who was washing the steps with a filthy rag. Delicately stepping over the spaces they thought she had washed, they climbed up past the reeking toilets to the skylit lobby where a younger woman washed the tiled floor with another filthy rag. She raised her head at their footsteps, recognized Mohammed, and scrambled to her feet. She greeted him excitedly in Arabic. Then, out of courtesy to his companion said, "Bonjour, Monsieur. Vôtre Oncle est au restaurant. Je lui appellerai."

"Non, merci," he said and explained something in Arabic. He was given two, Susan noted with relief, two keys.

"Over here. These are the best view." He opened the shutter doors into a large white room and the sea beyond. The coast curved around to an island, unclaimed except by a lighthouse and a mosque rising above the sandy hills.

"That's Torsa. We can go there tomorrow if you like." And perhaps fearing that "tomorrow" would make her weigh her time again, he made a more immediate suggestion. "See the Chalet restaurant there? Let's go see my uncle."

They walked through the dark bar which led into a small dining room where extradurable hotelware was arranged on heavy linen tablecloths. The room smelled of cigarette smoke and thick coffee and last night's bouillabaisse. Out on the patio, a man with a peppery Afro stared at the empty water.

He turned at their footsteps. "Mohammed. Mohammed!" he shouted. Inspecting Susan carefully, he smiled more broadly and said, "Bienvenue, Mademoiselle."

"Wrong language," laughed Mohammed, hugging the older man. "Claude, please meet my friend Susan Campbell from London and Canada and San Francisco."

"I am charmed. Well, Mohammed, perhaps you are not such a hopeless intellectual after all. Come, come, sit down, Susan. May I offer you a coffee?"

"Please, black," she said.

"So, so," mused Uncle Claude, examining her openly. Should she save him the trouble and declare outright that she was 128 pounds, five feet four inches, naturally brunette with six streaks of grey, able to swim thirty laps when her bad knee accommodated, normally good skin—the pimples and the four chin hairs being the result of her period? Perhaps he wouldn't be interested that she preferred an IUD to the pill.

Mohammed explained. "Susan is writing an article on North Africa for an English magazine. I told her I would show her the real Morocco."

"Ah, ha," said Claude. "It is an intellectual attachment."

Come on, she thought, I don't look like his bloody grandmother.

Claude turned to her sympathetically. "Mohammed is an incurable scholar. He talks only about his literature. A very backward boy. He has told you that we have surrendered and are sending him to America? Perhaps he will succeed where people are paid to think about thinking."

Mohammed sensed her aggravation.

"We just came over to say hello, Uncle Claude. And to tell you we took the two front rooms if that's OK."

Uncle Claude nodded benevolently.

"I thought I would take Susan for a walk on the scala, to see the village."

The wall was built by the Portuguese against the Spanish. Essaouira and El Jadida were the oldest relics of Portuguese colonization. It was a good lecture, the first time she had listened to Mohammed at length. She was amazed at how easily they got on, without any of the hostility she felt from most Moroccan men. He was, after all, ten years younger than her. Too young, perhaps, to feel threatened. He told her that the village had been captured by the Spanish, then the French and for a short time by the Germans. This accounted for the polyglot of street names and the families with blue eyes.

"My family was very lucky. My grandfather was the assistant to the French owner of a phosphate mine in Zagora. He was able to establish my father and his two brothers in their own businesses. When my parents died, my grandfather took me in and educated me. Scholarship is very highly prized here. You must not listen to Uncle Claude. The jokes are his way of being modest. He is very proud. It is a big honor for the family."

"And for yourself too? Does everything belong to the family? What do *you* want?"

"I'll learn that. Meanwhile I listen to other people, more

experienced people."

"You have to be careful. Really careful about this business of living your life for other people."

"Who do *you* live for?" he asked.

"Myself," she said.

"And is that enough?" he asked.

"No, not enough," she said.

The sun hung high. Wind fanned the usually relentless Moroccan humidity from the air. They listened to the shrieks of children in the medina below and the calls of the gulls gliding around the boats. Women wheeled carts of fish along the wharf toward the village. She felt a slight panic that she would lose the sensation by savoring it like this.

"I feel worn out from that early dash and the bus journey. I'd like to go back to the hotel this afternoon while you go and . . ." (Did she really want to say 'play'?) ". . . see your other friends."

◊

Now the room felt small and tawdry. The ocean was curtained off by a purple and pink synthetic spray of flowers. The white walls of this morning had retreated behind a functional plywood wardrobe, a chipped table and a filthy sink. The mauve plastic soap shelf was the newest accessory by twenty years. She curled up on the springless bed and took out the letter.

"So maybe I should give up on men my own age. And give up writing. I could run an apprenticeship program for young Arab pimps. Seriously, Hilary, this kid is all sinew and shine. Small tight ass and broad, solid shoulders. There's strength in every part of him. I'm scared whenever he opens his mouth that he's going to sound like my dopey little brother. I guess I have to admit that I have been turned on by a couple of kids back home. I feel guilty, not just lecherous, but perverted. Like I might defile this young, virgin flesh. Like the only reason he's interested in me is that he hasn't had any better offers. Like the only reason I'm interested in him is that I'm desperate. Horny. Old and horny.

"I contrive this lurid scenario where my withered flesh meets (meats) his well-toned skin. Perhaps that's what's bothering me. Rejection. Rejection by this young prick. Oh, hell. How did I get myself into this mess? Mother would charge me with nymphomania. Where is my self-respect, she would ask. And I must admit that lately I don't seem to be able to find it. I've lost all momentum to do anything—to keep on writing, to travel, to give up smoking. I feel like my life is overdue at the library and I can't get around to taking it back, so I leave it to collect fines of guilt in my head.

"Anyway, maybe all this angst about Mohammed is vanity. Maybe he only wants a seminar on American foreign aid or an orientation course for his career at Stanford. He has said nothing. Nothing except that he wants me to see Essaouira. Maybe I'm the old maid, scratching for flattery. I've got to get back to work. I'd like to get some good shots of the scala and the mosque has some fascinating Moorish inscriptions."

Susan was wakened by leaves fingering across her window. The tall tree looked like a hybrid palm-pine. She must ask Mohammed what kind it was. Running a trickle of lukewarm water from the faucet, she considered the grey porcelain. How could tourist hands get so dirty?

His door was ajar and her knock pushed it open. Mohammed was sitting on his single bed reading Matthew Arnold. She couldn't remember much. She liked *Calais Sands*. Maybe they could talk about it over dinner. She was starving.

The men shouted to them in Arabic and French the moment they walked onto the pier. "Sardine, Madame, Monsieur. Bon prix. Le meilleur." The chefs stood behind long wooden tables roasting the day's catch of sardine. Fishermen hunched over quick meals, gulping glasses of murky water. They were ignored for these new customers. One man waved a lobster. "Dix dirhams. Ten dirhams. Zehn dirhams." Who said the German coaches didn't get this far?

Mohammed's friend Paolo cooked up ten sardines and laid them on their plates, wide-eyed and oozing oil or vital fluids or both. She regarded the fish hopelessly, as the complete canned consumer. She didn't even know how to eat. He laughed at her and gently decapitated the specimen, then extracted the backbone. He showed her the flesh on the other side of the fish, too. Paolo squeezed lemon over it and told her to mop up the juices with a piece of bread. Mohammed and Paolo spoke in French so she could understand, but she was too absorbed in her meal to chat.

The next morning he took her to the medina. Susan found the spice stalls most appealing: glowing cayenne and paprika, the cologne of oregano. The tables of nuts seemed fresh, wholesome, real. The familiarity of the food was reassuring. She, as always, was seeing everything in comparison to the West. The mosques and schools were so different from the yawning steel and glass institutions at home. A high-pitched whine resonated behind them. Snake charmer? She turned into a darkened doorway. Inside sat rows of children droning the Koran.

"We have to know the Koran by the time we are sixteen," Mohammed said with nervous formality. "It is the basis of our cultural, religious and civic behavior."

She watched some small children playing outside their parents' jewelry shops. Peeking in a tapestry souk, she saw three men sitting around a pot of tea.

"So why don't you stay?" he asked.

"What was that you said about sand dunes," she said. "I would really like to get some shots of the coast."

Before they had walked a mile-and-a-half out of town, the wind erupted. The beach stretched between them and the ocean like a desert in a dust storm.

"The sand is terrible for my lens." She fastened the cap and shut the camera in the leather case. "That's really too bad," she said, shading her eyes and turning around toward the village.

"Come on. Let's take a walk as long as we're here. It's not often that you see North African sand dunes and a pirate's castle."

"A pirate's castle? How can I refuse?"

Mohammed had already slipped off his sandals and was

running across the beach. She followed, laughing and shouting for him to wait. He didn't turn back, just waved his hand over his head for her to follow.

Sun scorched the waves. The wind ballooned her blouse and quickened her feet. There was nothing on the beach except his feet making instantly disappearing tracks in the sand and her feet following. Nothing but miles and layers of sand. She had a sudden rush of freedom, exhilaration and fear.

It was an abrupt fall. She hadn't noticed that she was sinking until she struggled for thirty or forty seconds. Then it seemed to take him minutes to hear her calling, hours to come running back across the sand.

His voice was ages above her. It said not to fight. Stay still. Reach out for his hand. She sank further and further. Then there was a strap, a belt, which she caught and gripped. She felt something holding on to her. She saw the camera sinking in the quicksand. She saw it and thought, I ought to reach out and save it. Save it. I ought to. But she was too exhausted for anything except being held.

"Let's go and wash off all this grime," she heard a voice saying and followed him to the water.

They must have been lying on the beach for an hour before she awoke to find her head on his arm, her face toward the village. She didn't want to move. She didn't want to worry about how old she was, how old he was, what people would think, what she ought to think. Yesterday that anxiety had been impossible to see through or to write through. Now she turned to him and smiled wanly, wary of mirage.

"Do you feel well enough to walk?" he said.

"Yes," she said, surprising herself with laughter. "I want to see the pirate's castle."

The sun rode lower now, dodging behind the walls of the ruin. As they walked and ran a broken line across the sand, Morocco seemed miles behind them. The ship treading out there in the distance—Long John's or Matsui's—was their only company. Astonished by her energy, she climbed high to broken turrets. He chased her and she chased him around the outside. They caught each other and held on, laughing until they were both breathless. They kissed and held, like accomplices in a dream. The sun creased a thin red line between the pink sky and the ocean.

The sickness descended as they walked back to town. Susan threw up twice before they reached the hotel. Mohammed said not to worry. It was probably the fish. And the high wind. He wasn't feeling so well, himself. He ministered with toilet paper from her bag. They walked more and more slowly.

◊

It all went too slowly. Step after step. She had to be careful about where to place each foot, about which part of the foot to put down first, to see that her shoe didn't fall off. She lost patience, and fell out of step. The film picked up speed. She watched with panic. She could not get back inside the film. She was too tired, too old, too late. Now. She must do something NOW. But in Berkeley it was still yesterday and in the film it was already tomorrow. Where was now?

Now the ache at the back of her head seemed to encompass her brain. So many odd dreams. Eerie. She must try to remember. So many. So weary. Soooooo sick. Her whole being seemed filled with poison. She rushed to the sink and barely finished vomiting before she felt the pain of shit coursing to her rectum. He woke and drearily asked how she felt. She rushed out the door and down the hall to the toilet. Down to the smell of other soft movements, evidenced by the greenybrown tissues tossed in the stinking basket next to the toilet. She examined the color critically in comparison to her own. She was not, after all, alone. She answered his knock on the door cheerfully, as if she were expecting friends to tea. Fine. She was fine. Why didn't he go back to his own room? He needed his sleep. She would be fine on her own.

Susan spent the next four hours between her sink and the toilet. She tried to console herself by translating the multilingual graffiti, by gauging the pounds she was losing, by

planning her itinerary. She could pick up a secondhand Insta-
matic in Marrakech. She didn't want to leave him, but she
had to get going on the article. Maybe around American Express she could find a camera; kids were always running out
of money and selling things. Maybe Mohammed could do
some travelling with her. She had two weeks to get down to
the desert and back up to the Rif. He would enjoy being a
guide. And she could return the favor when he came to California; she could introduce him to her friends. They would
notice the change in her. She noticed it already.

His eyes were heavily shadowed, as if he were the one who
hadn't slept. She must tell him she was really all right. She
wasn't the sick tourist he saw. She was really all right.

"I think you ate something unfamiliar," Mohammed said
once again. "Probably the fish."

"I'll be OK," she whispered.

"If you're sure," he said. "I might go to see my cousin."

Susan considered his earnest face and tried not to see a
student asking permission to leave the room.

"I'll be fine alone," she said.

But after five minutes, she realized she didn't want to be
alone. So she pulled out the letter to Hilary.

"Sorry this has been so fragmented. Have decided to postpone menopause for a while. I'm no longer a hoary witch. I
know this will offend your feminist sensibilities, but this man
makes me feel so alive." Susan took frequent intermissions
at the sink and the toilet. It became harder and harder to continue. However, she needed to stay awake, away from the
nightmares. She had to sort it out now. She fought off the
drowsiness. If only Hilary could understand. If only she
could convince Hilary . . . .

"Mohammed makes me feel like I have a right to be young."
Hilary would have to agree that she shouldn't be ageist. And
anyway, what is young? Certainly not someone who has
moved all around North Africa since he was thirteen working
for different uncles and grandfathers. Not someone who has
enough determination to get an American scholarship. Not
someone gentle enough to sit up the entire night with me.

108

What is old? Susan could barely keep awake.

She imagined or saw or dreamed, *Hilary, lotus position in her jeans on a conveyor belt. Singing spirituals to the sisters in the factory. Giving the women a chance to rest while she's on the assembly line. Hilary reaches over and hugs Chrissie Moore. Gives Emma Dickson a male doll for the baby. Hands Maud the address of a safe abortionist. She raises her hands and conducts them in hymns of consciousness. She is approaching Susan. "All those who see the light step forward," she sings, "join me on the Kotex belt."*

"Come on, Susan, swim. Catch me. Come on, further out. Don't you have waves in California? Come on, just to the other side of the castle. Come on. Don't give up. Don't give up."

She woke up exhausted; vomited; shat; fell back into the race. *Different this time. The wind moved her. She never dreamed she would make it to the Olympics. Crowds were cheering. She thought they were cheering. She ran faster, but she still couldn't hear. She couldn't recognize the faces of the spectators now: Hilary, Mother, Mohammed, Guy, her little brother and a very young, unfamiliar boy were all waiting on the other side of the tape. Panic gripped her heart. Whom was she running against? Where was she running to? She could hardly breathe. What were they yelling? To go a different way? To speed up? To take longer strides? Where were the other runners? Maybe close behind. She would not turn around. Instead she kept her eyes ahead, looking past the spectators, looking beyond their mute faces, oblivious to everything except the power in her own legs. And the silence.*

Her legs ached. Everything ached when she awoke. But she no longer felt nauseated or cramped. Nothing left to vomit or shit. She was still tired, but *so* much better. Warm winds gathered outside, lapping the sidewalk with waves, splashing the flowers in and out of the open window.

Mohammed appeared out of nowhere with some boiled rice. He said she would be all right. His cousin, the doctor, said it was just the forty-eight hour tourist tummy. She would be all right.

Yes, she nodded, gobbling the rice with surprising appetite. She said she felt better already.

He put his arm around her shoulder and together they watched the still sleeping village. Two tourists, wearing irridescent orange backpacks, climbed the hotel steps. The maid wiped mucky circles with her rag. Otherwise, the streets were quiet. Wheelbarrows leaned against the scala. The pier was vacant of fishermen and sardine chefs. Ships bobbed lazily in the now crowded harbor. She kissed Mohammed and they lay back on the bed together.

Susan had been closed so long that she was afraid she was locked. But the slopes of his body smoothed her hands. The hard muscles of his calves gripped her thighs. His arms roped around her back. He hardened against her stomach and she allowed herself to want. They filled the bed with relief, joy, hunger, surprise. She had lied to herself, by herself, so long. Afterwards, he slept like he had not allowed himself to do during her illness. Susan lay awake, soothed by that even breathing.

And she played with a splinter of fear. Was this real? How long could it last? Would he make the rest of the trip with her? What would her mother say about all this weight she had lost? Would Hilary think she was a whore? "Whore!" "Hure!" "Putain!" Silence. She heard nothing. But she wasn't listening for the voices anymore. Or for the echoes. She heard nothing. Closing her eyes, she waited peacefully for the aroma of coffee and the crocketing of wheelbarrows from the street below.

Aunt Victoria

My Aunt Victoria came back from Moscow tonight. She is my favorite aunt, of all my mom's sisters, even though I have hardly ever seen her during the fifteen years of my life.

"Victoria is a dancer before and after everything else," my mother was explaining to my father, who doesn't like dancing, on the highway to JFK Airport. It was just mom and dad and me in the car because we knew Aunt Victoria would be tired after flying for so long. My mom was in a bad mood because she had just had a terrible fight with my sister Marie who had to stay home and babysit the younger kids.

"How come she gets to go?" Marie yelled, meaning me.

"Because she actually takes the time to write to your aunt," mom said.

Marie doesn't see much use in writing anything. She's seventeen and engaged to Kevin Cagney. So she called me a *prima donna,* and thinking I wouldn't know what it meant, she also called me, "teacher's pet." Of course I told her she was just jealous. Then my mom told me to keep still or I wouldn't get to go either.

My dad hates the ride to JFK. "What does being a dancer got to do with us turning our lives upside down when she comes?" he wanted to know.

"She's an artist," said my mom. "She needs the right conditions. She would go crazy trying to find her way on the airport bus."

"She's crazy altogether," he said. "She's too nervous to look into your eyes when she talks. And she's always yapping about London or Paris or some goddamned place you never heard of. What's she coming home for anyway?"

I could have answered them that. I just got a letter from her last week. She always writes on blue vellum with black ink.

But my mom was talking already. "Oh, dear, when Victoria called, it was such a garble. She said she just wanted to see us all. She said that we, meaning the two of us, would go up to Manhattan to see a ballet together."

"Swell," he said. "We're the limousine so Ms. Big Shot can do her business. Last time she dropped by America, she didn't even fucking bother to call."

"She was just in Washington for one benefit performance," mom said. "And will you please watch your language."

"Listen, the more Susie Q. in the back seat there knows, the less likely she'll grow into . . . ."

"She's shy," I said, and I was going to tell him how much Aunt Victoria missed us, too, but my mom told me to be quiet and not to interrupt my father.

When we saw Aunt Victoria at the airport, she didn't look very shy or lonely. She looked like an empress. Her hair was piled high with silver combs. She was wearing a red velvet skirt

112

and a beautiful black shawl with flowers on it. She talked all the way home in the car and after dinner she gave everybody presents. She brought mom and dad a samovar and Marie a painted box and I'm really excited because she brought me a shawl just like hers—black with flowers. When mom sent us all to bed, dad seemed happier. He was drinking vodka and listening to Aunt Victoria's funny stories about Russian toilets.

I can still hear them laughing from the living room. Mom said it was all right to sit up late and write, if I didn't tell my sister Marie. And she told me we should put away the shawl for a couple of years. She said it was a little too dark for someone only fifteen years old.

IX
Aerogramme

Dear Susan,

Drizzling here. I'm approaching that London dilemma of whether to risk the fumes of my gas fire or bear the cold a while longer. God, I envy your California respite. We've all missed you terribly these last months.

Even Pia misses Susan, but that's more than she'd admit to me. Of course, Pia is what Susan wants me to write about. How is Pia? Why hasn't Pia sent more than a postcard? Listen, none of us counted on much more from Pia. Once we had hoped she would go back to the States with Susan. At least for a time. For her own sake. Susan and the sun would have kept her much warmer than the Dutch gin.

I was delighted when they got together. Thought it would be good therapy for Pia and it might purge Susan of some innocence. Every woman I know who's had a lesbian affair in London has been with our Pia. For Susan, though, it turned out to be much more than an affair. It *was* Susan's turn. Or mine, but I decided a long time ago that I'm basically asexual. Anyway, I had seen their affair coming for a while. Even had something to do with it. A few initial phone calls, if you know what I mean. And I did bring Susan to Sara's wedding, which is the night she first slept with Pia.

Sara's wedding was Mardi Gras for sure. The last fling. Touches of celebrity. Made *Londoner's Diary* because Sara was "The West End Feminist." The newspapers weren't the only place Sara was panned for "giving in and getting married." Anyway, we all wore black—all her friends—completely without collusion. Well, Pia always wore black. But that night everyone did. Even Susan, who was forever tented in those North African reds and oranges. She hung up her Goulimime beads for a long silver chain. Sara, in her flowered Liberty cotton, was too pissed on Daddy's champagne to notice the mourning tones when we all paraded in at ten p.m. She didn't notice Pia's strained charm turn to wild dancing turn to intimate chat about the scars of Catholic daughterhood with Susan.

Was I the only one who knew that Susan had been in love with Pia for nine months, ever since Susan came to our Women's Socialist Literature Collective?

Looks like we have a nibble for the book. Virago says they can do a run of 7,000 paperback. Your photos are fine. I'm actually getting off on being a literary agent. I'd give up the PR job altogether if I could find enough feminist clients.

Our collective was more than an editorial group. For some of us, it was Bloomsbury. For Sara, it was a revolutionary citoyenne brigade. For Pia, it was a CP lit caucus, descended from the thirties. Like so many of the progressive groups in London now, it was half North American. Why did we stay in Britain when the pound was falling, the postboxes were being blown up, and everyone was going on strike? Well, because a lot of us had studied English literature. We figured if we wanted to write literature, we had to be in England. *Un peu naïve,* you might say, but that idealism was the very best part of all of us.

It's odd that Susan, despite all her other quixotic ideas, never had any illusions about being "a writer." She had come to London as a reporter. As a photographer and journalist. She said she would take pictures and do reviews for us, but forget this creative writing business. Superbly realistic, she seemed, and very young. The brightest one of us, for sure. My five years here haven't cured me of what my British mates call "individualism." I still place friends in some high school yearbook. "Most Likely to Succeed." That was Susan, because of all of us, she knew what she wanted to succeed *at.* Pia qualified as "Most Popular" and, as I gradually understood, also "Most Innocent."

Why do I keep coming back to Pia? Perhaps because her vulnerability brings out the mother in everyone. As Moira says, "feminism stimulates lactation." Of course, one look at Pia and most mothers would run the other way with their arms locked across their breasts. She is almost frighteningly gorgeous with that bobbed, hennaed hair, those antique silk blouses and Hepburn slacks. She usually wears funky pumps or black espadrilles and a coke spoon on a silver chain around her neck. Women in the collective were always teasing about the sexism in her dress.

"What do you mean?" Pia declared after one meeting. "I'm the biggest raving dyke here."

"But you still dress like some man's fantasy," Susan said.

"Why some man's?"

Susan blushed. She really was young sometimes, or maybe just honest.

"And who are you geared up to be?" asked Pia. "Jill Johnston's fantasy in your loose sweaters and always jeans? That's an image, too, you know. Why the hell do you bind your hair in that leather noose? You look like some vegetarian nun."

Susan let it pass, partially because she was beginning to be seduced and partially because Susan always respected people with *reasons* who had thought out their positions. They disagreed desperately on Doris Lessing that night. Pia said Lessing was too worthy, too moral. Now, her idea of an expatriate was Anaïs Nin. Susan charged Pia with having a patriarchal aesthetic and they had a terrible fight.

Great to hear you're doing so well in San Francisco. How's the job? Does California feel any different now that you're an editor? Are you being smothered by good old Yankee provincialism? We were all over at Pia's last night comparing letters from you, our prodigal sister. We all *miss you a lot.*

On the night of Sara's wedding, I had arranged to stay over with a friend—just in case Susan wanted the flat to herself, just in case anything happened with her and Pia. At midnight, they were drinking Sara's daddy's champagne from the same glass and talking about a Holly Near album. A half hour later, they were missing from the party.

The next afternoon, Susan told me the story. I was quite proud of Susan for taking the initiative. After hearing the first side of the album and half of the second Pia said, "Not as hokey as I expected. I like it."

"And I like *you*," said Susan, taking her hand.

"This isn't going to work out, honey," Pia told her. "It never works out with straight women. I'm just intermission."

"We'll see about that."

Susan said the sex was wonderful, a real turn-on. For me, it's pretty much an aesthetic appreciation. I've always thought women's bodies were more beautiful. I fell in love with Isadora Duncan when I was twelve and with Vanessa Redgrave ten years later. Evidently, however, Pia's initiation wasn't as delicate as I had imagined.

"You don't have to do that, you know," Pia said. "Straight women always think they've got to come down on you the first time."

"Pia, this is wonderful."

"Yeah, doll, it's OK for me, too."

Remember Susan had wanted to be with her for almost a year.

"Pia, I think I'm in love."

"Don't say that."

That meeting at Pia's was the first time we all got together since you left. Everyone has been frantically chasing around on this Agee-Hosenball CIA stuff. If the Home Office deports them, I'm leaving. I may not have much choice. They're searching peoples' flats. Someone took Jenny's address book from her car seat. The government is tightening ass every- where. It's scary. With the pound this far down, people are going frantic politically—turning Tory or Commie. More Tory.

Pia and Susan had always gone to the same meetings, parties and marches. Now they would be going together. Their debut was Jenny's Ph.D. celebration. Jenny had broken off with Pia three months before. Pia had seriously thought about marrying Jenny and following her off to Kenya. Now Jenny was going to Lake Rudolf on her own. Pia hadn't told her about Susan yet and she was clearly agitated as we rode the cab from Holloway to Lexham Gardens. Susan held her hand and chatted with me happily.

Amazing how unself-conscious Susan was. Their affair scared Pia, I know. Too easy, she thought. Susan didn't know her well enough yet, Pia told me. Or maybe Susan couldn't find anyone else. Pia was accustomed to, and probably enjoyed, breaking down the tensions of shy, frightened or coy straight women. And here sat Susan, publicly—almost relentlessly—holding her hand.

You could feel the approval when they walked into the room. Pia's black silk elegance was accented by Susan's stunning cinnamon overalls. Jenny embraced them both and led them over to the wine table where Pia downed a bottle of Graves Burgundy during a fifteen minute conversation about clitoridectomies among the Masai.

Pia asked Susan if she'd like to bop. Susan, still on her first glass of wine, said she was a klutz. But soon they were swinging, Pia's slacks flouncing, to Bill Haley and his Comets. Pia sashayed into the drapes and managed to bring the rod down on their heads. Of course Susan was hurt, too, but she was considerably more sober.

Pia spent the rest of the evening lying in Susan's lap, eating pâté, and chatting to the visitors. She hadn't looked that relaxed in a year.

Pia has been doing some work for the Guardian *arts section. Fringe theatre reviews and a couple of interviews. She says you can do more in the union if you're working for a mainstream paper. You must have had some impact on her, you little bourgeois reformer.*

They were really good for each other. It made me happy

just to have breakfast with them in the morning. Studious, practical Susan became almost frivolous. Pia felt more secure than she had in ages.

Together they worked closely on the abortion campaign, the feminist aesthetics conference, the union. Alistair called them "the Bobbsey Twins" which Susan hated because it reminded Pia they were both American.

"Even if you were Canadian, it wouldn't be so bad," Pia told her. "But it's like waking up with a mirror sometimes. You're everything I tried to escape—broad American accent, orthodontic straight teeth, rampant freckles."

Pia had worked damn hard at getting away from West Hollywood High. She took the first train to Bennington and couldn't get out of the States fast enough when she got that offer from The Hogarth Press.

"I knew I would never make it as an all-American girl," she told Susan. "I found the culture so stifling. I wasn't wholesome enough."

"And I'm Miss USA?" said Susan.

"You're sweet enough."

"I suppose I'd be more interesting if I had a heroin habit or was into bondage."

"I suppose you would."

"I love you. Isn't that enough?"

"Maybe too much," frowned Pia. "Don't talk like that."

You asked about Shana in the last letter. She's the artist whom Pia has been seeing. They're still "together," if that's the word. It's been three months now. Perhaps they've stuck it out because Shana's always away. She's not very good to Pia. She sees other people, including Jenny, who still hasn't split for Lake Rudolf. Pia has been drinking more lately, expensive Dutch gin that Shana brings back duty-free from her tours. She's getting thinner, smoking more. I don't want to guilt trip you or anything. You made the right choice in going back to the States. But you were so good for her.

Actually, I had known Pia two years before Susan phoned me from Victoria Station, said she was a friend of my sister's, and asked if she could spend the night on my couch. She wound up staying years. Yes, I was quite in the middle of their relationship in a lot of ways. Mother to Pia, confidante to Susan. Interesting, I thought I knew Pia until Susan told me about their conversation on fantasies.

"So if I'm Miss USA," said Susan, "who are you? Don Juan in Hell?"

"No, I hate Shaw, too snide," said Pia.

"Not Mr. Darcy?"

"No, *not* Mr. Darcy."

"Well, it's got to be romantic," said Susan.

"Oh, definitely romantic," said Pia as she rolled over and played with Susan's long curls. "How would you feel about Peter Pan?"

I told Susan, later, that she made a good Wendy, certainly a much better one than I. I never had Susan's capacity for involvement. Sure, I admit I was in love with both of them and scared to death of it. Like my Aunty Jane, who's a smalltime dance impressario in Brooklyn, I'm more given to secondhand adventures. Obviously both Susan and Pia understood that.

Spare Rib wants to excerpt your essay for their January issue. They can't pay, of course. And they all ask about you.

That *Spare Rib* party was probably the beginning of the end for Susan and Pia. It was like an anniversary of the women's movement in London. Everyone was there. Sara wore black this time, one of those sensuous voile blouses with satin slacks. Spectacular. This was the first time we'd all been together since her wedding.

Funny, five years ago we were all novices and now we were professional feminists. Leah ran the Women's Studies Centre at Warwick. Kate had started Scottish Women's Aid. Moira, after an outrageous three year affair with Pia, had married a rabbi and founded a literacy project for women in Slough. Susan had been offered this magazine job in San Francisco.

Susan was alternately jubilant and tormented about the job. I know she would have stayed in London if Pia had asked.

But Pia was dancing with everybody else that night.

I'm still toying with the idea of going back to the States, myself. You're a good example for me. I do miss it. I miss people with the same sense of humor, whose accents I understand the first time around. I'm tired of never having enough meat and of getting the flu twice every winter. I sometimes even miss my mother. But if I left England, I would miss the Half Moon Theatre, the King's Head Pub, the terrible jokes in Private Eye. *How could I leave my friends here?*

They went to Brighton to settle their future. Whitsun at Bobbie's. I thought it was a bad idea because Bobbie can be overbearing and, besides, she's been in love with Pia for years. But she was gracious, apparently. Served them Asti Spumanti in bed. And except for Sunday brunch, when she went into a tirade about the politics of semiotics, Bobbie stayed in the background.

They spent the weekend sleeping late and noshing at those little cafés on the waterfront. Susan said they had never been that close. She would stay awake at night, just for the sense of Pia's arms around her. She didn't say she loved Pia. She hadn't said that in months. She thought Pia might say it now. All Pia really had to say was "Stay."

She didn't. On Sunday night, during their second bottle of Pouilly Fuissé. Susan said she had to decide about whether she would go to San Francisco.

"Look," said Pia. "I don't want to be responsible for anyone's life."

"But loving someone is a responsibility."

"Susan, I don't like being pushed."

"Who's pushing?"

"You are, damn it. You always are. By being too kind. Too loving. You're a good person, Susan."

"And what's wrong with that?"

Pia always got angry when she felt guilty and she shouted back now, "I'll tell you what's wrong with that. It's not very *interesting.*"

Are you still thinking about coming back for the summer?

*Moira says she can get a cottage at the Lakes for a week, or
something at the Yorkshire Downs. Pia was glad to hear you
were coming.*

They were together for Susan's last night in London. The
next morning, Susan almost missed her plane because Pia
couldn't find her briefcase. She bumped her head as we all
jumped in the taxi to go to the West London Air Terminal.
That seemed to break the tension and we laughed and exchanged last minute messages to friends in the States.

"The book?" said Susan. "My copy of the manuscript,
what did you do with it, Pia?"

"I don't have it. I thought Moira was supposed to get it
to you."

"So what's this?" said Susan. "The collective unconscious-
ness?"

Pia leaned into Susan's arms, laughing and promising to post
it to her the next day. It was the first time I had ever heard
her volunteer to do clerical labor. As a matter of fact, I wound
up doing it myself, a week later.

The morning was grey. Buses at King's Cross belched filth.
The taxis clogged up Regent Street. Tourists trudged around
Picadilly Circus with hundreds of pigeons.

Susan said, "I've never understood what all the people saw
in Picadilly Circus."

"The Bovril sign, of course," said Pia. "Too bad the stuff
tastes so foul, but the sign is superb. Have you seen it in the
Lowry painting?"

"I haven't even seen it on top of that building before," admitted Susan.

"Listen honey," said Pia, "come to London sometime and
I'll show you around."

Susan insisted that Pia and I stay in the taxi because we
were both late for work. There was some joke at the end,
some sardonic comment of Pia's. I don't remember anything
except the laughing and the kissing and Susan loping off to
the ticket counter under her khaki rucksack like a goddamned
Girl Scout.

Pia began sobbing immediately. By the time we hit Earl's Court, it was definitely valium hour.

The cabbie, who looked like he had coped with a lot of avant garde dramas, turned and said feebly, "It's all right, luv, she'll come back. They always do."

"No they don't," Pia shot back. "They always grow up."

So anyway, Susan, let me know when your schedule is firm. I'll meet you. Actually, you should let Pia know your plans, too. I'm not trying to choreograph anything, but why don't you just drop her a postcard? All the sisters miss you. Love, Carol.

One of Them

"They've taken over Women's Studies," said the History Professor.

"They certainly make my wedding ring feel heavy," said the Associate Dean of Students.

"Always acting 'more feminist than thou,' " said the Poet-In-Residence.

Cornelia regarded her friends and realized this was a party of well-known feminists. Scholars who had taken risks for their politics. Some who always had a "gut feeling" for feminism. Women who had found Charlotte Perkins Gilman. Who wrote books about the tyranny of motherhood. And all of them "struggling" on the home front, too, with their bullheaded men. Almost all of them.

Naturally the conversation turned to lesbians. Cornelia understood why. The woman wearing the fedora had walked out into the garden. Cornelia listened to their complaints and imagined the garden as some sort of wild game refuge.

"They judge your feminism on your bed partner," said Barbara.

"Who does that?" asked Cornelia.

"Andrea Dworkin," interrupted Rose angrily, "says heterosexual sex is murder."

"It's their attitude that bothers me," shot Kim. "Like the aggressiveness of their clothes."

Cornelia knew these women well. Knew they appreciated irony. Self-irony. "There's a uniform?" she smiled.

Barbara looked past her, responding to Kim. "And the almost bragging display of affection." She stabbed a strawberry and grape together with her toothpick.

"I heard of a woman at Smith," whispered Rose, "who slept her way to the top of her department and it didn't have anything to do with phallic power."

"So lesbians are running the American university system?" asked Cornelia, still betting on humor. She tried to ignore the migraine starting behind her left eye.

Mariette considered Cornelia cautiously, obviously worrying her friend would do something rash. Even breathing too deeply in your year of tenure could be rash.

"Cornelia," said Kim, "you can't deny that in some places it's easier to be 'woman-identified,' as they so self-righteously put it."

"Stop it," said Mariette. "Stop bickering about who's more oppressed."

"They're the ones," said Barbara, filling everyone's wine glass, "who brand you with your personal life."

"But think of all the lesbians who are still in the closet," said Cornelia, feeling her body temperature rise ten degrees, "who are afraid to lose their jobs."

"At our school?" laughed Rose. "At good old Progressive U?"

"The real stigma," said Barbara, "is the nepotism rule. Do you know how hard it is to be married to someone in the same field?"

"Yes," Kim began, "when I was at Hopkins . . . ."

Cornelia looked closely at the faces of her friends, her colleagues, her sisters and wondered how well she knew them, despite all the committee meetings and potlucks and commiserating drinks. Sometimes she felt like a hypocrite for not coming out to them. Other times she was sure they all knew. But for five years she had been silent. ("Self-protective," she called it. "Paranoid," charged Ruth. "Reserved," said Karen. "Sensible," said Mariette, who was now monitoring her every breath.)

"They just won't let you be a feminist," said Rose. "Heterophobia, I call it. Unless you wear a flannel shirt and . . ." she paused, not wanting to sound too bizarre, "handcuffs or something . . . ."

Cornelia cleared her throat.

Mariette watched fearfully.

"You just don't understand," Cornelia began.

"Yes," interrupted Mariette, desperate to swerve her friend from self-destruction. "That's like calling blacks 'racists.' "

Cornelia could hear her own fear in Mariette's voice. And this woke her to the absurdity of hiding political choice from her allies.

"You don't understand," she said. "*I* am a lesbian." Cornelia's eyes met Barbara's for a moment before her friend became absorbed by a speck in her wine glass. "I am one of those dyke feminists and I haven't kept you from anything." She saw Rose inch away toward the wall. "If I had so much power, I would have come out years ago." She noticed the quavering in her voice and the shaking of her glass, which she set on the table. Looking around, she found Mariette was the only one looking at her.

"I think what Cornelia's done is very brave," said Mariette.

"Oh, yes," said Rose. "I know how you feel. Remember when I lived with that heroin addict for a while? The stigma, I understand stigma."

"And discreet," said Barbara. "We've known you for four, five years! It's a real tribute to your social skills."

"How about a real indictment of social prejudice," said Mariette bitterly.

"Of course, in the larger academy," said Rose. "But among us, well, I'm sure we all would have, well, sympathized."

Cornelia's migraine had reached her right eyebrow.

The garden doors opened, admitting the hatted woman.

"I mean," said Kim, lowering her voice, "it's not like you're really one of them."

X

Feel No Evil

Susan was reading Sheila Rowbotham. She was always reading while she waited and waiting to read while she wasn't. She got this from her mother who also read all the time. Not Sheila Rowbotham, but junk stuff like Anya Seaton, Frances Parkinson Keyes and Taylor Caldwell. Authors they displayed in the window of the American Opinion Library, for god's sake. It was like food, Susan sometimes thought, like her snobbishness about Mother's food. Whenever she visited that tiny, hot apartment, her mother fed her pork chops and fried potatoes with a big, healthy chunk of corn bread for dessert. Then Susan would spend the next two weeks cleaning herself with fruit and bran, confident that she would be a better person after a good dose of brewer's yeast.

Because she was reading, Elizabeth saw Susan before Susan saw her. Susan had arrived early to find a place by the window, a post, but now it was Elizabeth who was on guard.

Why had they picked the Skylight Room? Because the convex mirrors and heated hors d'oeuvres were *so* much not their milieu that they could regard the meeting as a vignette? Because they might fulfill their fantasies of chucking each other down twenty-four stories?

Susan recalled what Joan Didion had said about people with self-respect: "They know the price of things. If they choose to commit adultery, they do not then go running, in an access of bad conscience, to receive absolution from the wronged parties . . . ."

Susan had been away from Toronto for three years. Still, she was startled by the changes in Elizabeth. Her old friend looked harder, tenser, stonier, also younger. She wore the same innocent face, resolutely, painfully innocent. Sister Sans Charity.

Elizabeth's voice sounded familiar. "On second thought," she said, "I don't think it was such a good idea to meet. But I guess we can make this brief."

Susan nodded.

She noticed that Elizabeth was wearing that terrible, cheap Eaton's basement blouse with the blue and green ethereal flora. She must have remembered how much Susan hated the blouse. And those grey cords. Sloppiness still seemed a moral imperative of the women's movement in North America. Elizabeth sat on the edge of the booth and sloughed off her peacoat.

It was Susan's turn. Susan's turn to explain why she had phoned after all this time abroad, to explain just what she wanted.

"We were friends for a long time," Susan began, "you and Mike and Guy and I. We were like family. In fact, knowing my family, you were closer." Susan was embarrassed by the pleading in her voice, the obsequiousness. "We shared so much together."

Elizabeth remained silent.

"If you and Mike hadn't been sponsoring draft resisters," she said, gratefully, remembering the loneliness of those first days in Canada, "I don't know what Guy and I would have done."

"Probably divorced a lot sooner."

Susan wasn't going to forfeit their friendship to cheap pot shots. If it was going to end, it would have to be in a mighty explosion right here at this Upper Canadian cocktail lounge.

"Elizabeth, you were very important to me. You introduced me to all those women's books. We spent so many evenings drinking. We shared so much."

"Including Mike."

Susan noticed that she said, "including Mike," instead of "including my husband." Elizabeth never used the word "husband," as if they had got unmarried. She always introduced Mike as "the man I live with." She had changed her name back to Moreau (probably claiming to be Quebeçoise as well as single). But what did she know of being alone? Sometimes Susan hated married feminists, women for whom equal wages was a question of ethics rather than practicality, for whom independence was only a psychological state. And with Mike's good salary as a primatology professor, Elizabeth's survival was guaranteed.

"Yes, we all hurt each other a lot," Susan said.

"Hold on, you were the one . . . ."

"I was only one of the ones. You knew all along that Mike and I were fucking. You just never let on. You used our guilt against both of us."

"I did not," said Elizabeth. "I didn't know until the day you left for England."

"And it came to you in a blinding flash of light?"

"More like a blinding rage." Elizabeth smiled in spite of herself. "Tell me how you could have done it? How could you have pretended to be my friend—even giving me advice about my marriage—when you were sleeping with Mike?"

"If you criticize me for anything," said Susan nervously, "it should be for lack of originality in sleeping with my best friend's husband."

"Don't dismiss it with your articulate cynicism, Susan. You were using real people. With real feelings. I was hurt and angry. I'm still very angry."

"And hurt?"

"And hurt."

Susan stopped herself, remembering that sarcasm had always been one of her more refined defenses. And now, although she kept telling herself she didn't want Elizabeth's forgiveness, Susan felt the fullness of this want for the first time in three years.

"It was so confusing," Susan said. "There were so many

lies going down at the end. And then I left. You don't understand what was happening."

"I understand why you left, all right. I just don't get why you came back."

The cocktail waitress, costumed in an ass-high red petticoat, approached. "May I serve you ladies another?"

Susan had been watching Elizabeth's Dubonnet for signs of movement, hoping that she would want a second drink, that she would want more time together.

"No thank you," said Elizabeth, crunching on a piece of ice.

Susan ordered another beer. God, she was still making all the moves. It had always been like this. She was tempted to make an acerbic comment about the waitress' costume but that would have been an easy claim on their wounded sisterhood.

"I came back because we're all still alive. I thought we had a lot to give each other."

"Well, I haven't got any more books to recommend. Or any more husbands to lend."

"Oh, hell," Susan stood up. "I've got to go to the bathroom. If you're so sure it's dead, why don't you take this opportunity to eat your last piece of ice and leave?" Elizabeth just stared as she walked away. It had always been like this, Susan thought again, Elizabeth the watcher. She could make her living betting on people, especially people like Susan who always seemed to be racing.

She barely made it. So much for beer, she thought, consumed by the sweet relief of pissing, letting it all out, feeling empty, relaxed. She wondered how much bile there was in urine. Damn, she had not come to apologize. Hadn't she worked that out with herself over the past three years?

Elizabeth was sipping a fresh glass of Dubonnet.

"OK," said Elizabeth, summoning a conviction in which they both needed to believe. "Let's get a few things straight. Do you know why I was angry with you rather than with Mike when I understood—well, admitted—what was happening? Because I always felt as if I were competing for attention."

"That's bullshit," Susan said and then softened her voice. "Mike *loved* you; he needed your gentleness."

"Not competing with you for Mike, but with Mike for *you*. I always loved *you*, Susan."

Susan's disbelief was dissolved by Elizabeth's tense smile.

"I admired you, Susan, wanted to *be* you. It wasn't because of what Mike saw in you, but what I saw. I wanted you to love me."

Susan's cheeks flushed. She wondered if this was what she had wanted to hear from Elizabeth, what she wanted to give in return. But she did not know the territory of such a love. She was frightened and she bristled.

Susan told herself that she was crazy to be webbed by this vindictive wife. One minute, Elizabeth was wrapping her arms around her. The next minute would come the sting of retribution. Did black widow spiders practice on each other before killing the males? She refused to be trapped by any more guilt.

"Don't you see?" said Elizabeth bravely. "I felt that of all my friends you had something. Mike and I both thought so. He called it 'passion.' I knew I would never have it. At root, I'm an analyst. For the first year we all lived together, I coveted your passion. But believe me, it had nothing to do with Mike. When my thesis started to take off, I no longer needed to be you. But I did still need you."

"Oh, Elizabeth, if you only knew how much I admired your discipline."

This was clearly the wrong thing to say, Susan realized as she watched Elizabeth's face lose shape for a moment.

Elizabeth interceded, herself, "And when I found out you were screwing him, not only did I know I had lost you, but Mike, too."

Susan reached her hand across the table. Her small, cuticle-chewed, heavily-ringed fingers held Elizabeth's competent piano hand for a couple of minutes. They sat wordlessly. Susan started to cry.

"A week?" Elizabeth asked calmly.

131

"What?" Susan sniffed.

"You're only going to be here in Toronto a week?"

"Yes, my magazine job starts next month. I wish we had longer."

"Mike wants to see you."

"Well, I was hoping," Susan said hesitantly, "that we might all have supper together one night."

"He'd like to see you alone."

"No, I don't think that's a hot idea. There's too much room for misunderstanding. And too little time."

"But you and I have met alone."

Was Susan hearing this right? Was Mike's wife arranging an assignation with his ex-lover? Susan felt the same gut fear she had felt six years before when Mike found them all that cabin together, and later when he encouraged Elizabeth and herself to join a CR group. Sometimes, when her regret turned to bitterness, she wondered whether Mike regarded them with the same fascination as his experimental monkeys.

"But it was different for you and me," Susan said. "We should have met ages ago."

"He'll be really upset," said Elizabeth. "He says there are some things he needs to work out. Can't you see him for just one drink?"

"Working things out would take longer than one drink. I don't want any more misunderstandings."

Elizabeth regarded Susan, her fondness set on an edge of fear. "It's OK. We've all grown up a lot in the last couple of years."

"Well, maybe I am being paranoid," Susan paused, recalling how defensiveness had got the better of her several times this afternoon. Besides, what could happen after three years? "OK, I'll meet him for a drink on the night we all have supper together."

◇

Mike invited her to meet him at the lab. He wanted her to see Lyndon, his prize monkey, and to show her how much the facility had expanded. He had been offered a job in a bigger hospital, but he had turned it down to continue working with his favorite monkeys. After she made her way past the elaborate system of buzzers and locked doors, she could see him through the glass wall, inserting a dish of fruit into the cage. Succulent peaches, mangoes, pears and bananas.

Susan had planned to come bouncing in, saying something urbane and clever. However, she was so overwhelmed by the seductive, almost overripe fruit, and by the crazy, shitty monkeys, that all she could say was, "Hello, there."

"Oh, hello," Mike said.

He was uncharacteristically flustered, the director lost on his own set.

Susan noticed his hair was greyer. He wore the same shaggy Pendleton shirt. The jeans were tighter. He had gained weight in his thighs. A little disgusted by the flab, she was also relieved to find him fallible.

Following this scrutiny, he finally caught her in his eyes. Those eyes. No, those eyes hadn't changed. They were the same clouded blue eyes as that night he came up to her study and said, "You know, one of the reasons we argue so much, one of the reasons there is so much energy behind it, is the sexual tension." She had thought she was spellbound. As it turned out, he wasn't Svengali, but simply the first man she had slept with after her husband. He had used pop psychology, not hypnosis. He talked to her about "open marriages" and "meaningful relationships." And, gazing into his romantic eyes, she had chosen to rationalize with him.

"Funny place for a reunion," she laughed.

He nodded affectionately.

"Let's take a walk," she said, anxious for fresh air. "Through the leaves in Queen's Park. I haven't seen autumn for years."

"Sure. Sure. But aren't you forgetting to say hello to someone? This is Lyndon." He held out the monkey. "Bet you didn't recognize him. He's completely different from when you left."

"Absolutely. Hi, there, Lyndon. What's new with you?"

Mike nervously finished the feedings, rummaged around for his overcoat, piled student reports in his briefcase on top of the *Newsweek*. The *Newsweek* was some kind of prop. He never used to read *Newsweek*. And there was no subscription label on this one. It stuck out conspicuously.

"Good piece on Paisley this week," he said. "Of course I don't have the background on Ulster you do. God, those pictures of Ireland you did a couple of months back were impressive. We couldn't believe it was *our* Susan."

"Yes, I guess I learned a lot," she said, hating herself for the false modesty. Not that Mike expected her to say more. Thoroughly absorbed with Lyndon, he eased the monkey into an Adidas carrier bag.

Nauseous, Susan felt nauseous. The monkey shit, Mike's awkwardness, her naïveté. She would not throw up. How could she have taken Mike so seriously a few years ago? How had this man dictated her feelings—and Elizabeth's? Urgently, Susan wished it were all over, that she could get on the train going west and read, work on her book, write a letter, go to sleep. For now, she would concentrate on not throwing up.

"What time does Elizabeth want us back for dinner?" She asked as they walked toward Queen's Park.

"She said not to worry, any time between seven and eight."

"Oh," Susan said, uncomfortable with the notion of a wife fixing dinner. She tried to think of it as a friend fixing dinner.

"I knew you would come back," he was saying. "But why now?"

"Because it's the fall," she said, feeling pleased with herself. The fresh air felt good. She knew she would not throw up. "Because autumn is the best time for me. Because I wanted to crunch leaves beneath my feet again."

He was silent.

"You had something to say?" she asked.

"No, nothing particular."

"I mean, Elizabeth told me you had something to say to me."

"Oh, yes," he said, glancing around at the other walkers, all guaranteed in knit caps and mufflers against the first winter winds. He fixed his stare on the statue of Queen Victoria.

"I feel if you, Elizabeth and I are going to be real friends," he said, "we've got to proceed with total honesty. With all that we feel for each other."

"One evening doesn't give us much time," she said cautiously.

"I feel I have to tell you that I still have, and probably always will have, some very positive feelings for you."

Susan stopped and turned to him abruptly. "You spent ten years studying psychology and three more years being analyzed and this is the way you express yourself?" She thought she might be even more angry at what he was doing to words than at what he was doing to her.

"I love you, Susan, and I've told Elizabeth this."

"Oh, hell," said Susan.

Lyndon was making nonsense in the bag. Mike quickly unzipped it and slipped him a doggie biscuit.

"If you can't face it. . . ." he said.

Susan didn't hear the rest. It was starting to snow, just a light flurry, but she felt terribly cold.

"The only thing I want to face right now," she said, "is a hot-buttered rum. Why don't we go over to Maloney's?"

The cocktail lounge was dark and smoky with a heartier brand of tobacco than she was used to in London. Maybe the pungency came from American cigarette paper, which was heavier. The sour smell of lager was missing here, too, replaced with the heavy sweetness of bourbon and faded aftershave. She loved the pubs in London, especially the Freemason's Arms on Long Acre where her friends used to drink before union meetings. She hated North American cocktail lounges papered with the dull accomplishments of insurance salesmen and bank executives. Still, she had the sense that being comfortable in a place like this was what it meant to be grown-up.

He was talking. "Like I tell Elizabeth, we've all grown up

a lot in the last few years." For twenty minutes, he fiddled with his digital watch, talking not so much to her as to an idea. He said he always knew she would come back. He wanted to hear all about Mozambique and her union work and her friends and lovers.

She tried to explain to him what had happened to her and what she had done. But it all came out like mug shots in a photo booth, the flash bulb catching her worrying between the smiles.

Elizabeth and I always knew we could say, "We knew Susan Campbell when. . . ."

"Speaking of Elizabeth, hadn't we better get back?"

He looked at his watch, "My god, yes, it's almost 7:30."

"I thought you said it didn't matter."

"Oh, it doesn't," he said. "It doesn't, but you know this snow is going to make a longer trip than we expected. She'll understand."

This reminded Susan of what Elizabeth was meant to understand, the "positive feelings." Why was she so goddamned worried about Elizabeth? Elizabeth had everything—her work, her comfortable conscience, her husband. They could still hold on to each other at night.

◊

Elizabeth didn't exactly answer the door, but she did open it.

Susan handed her the bottle of Muscadet which she had expensively selected. While Mike took Lyndon in another room, she followed Elizabeth into the kitchen.

"How did your teaching go today?" Susan asked. It was the wrong thing to say, forced. She could see that now. Of course it was bloody forced. The air was palpable between them.

Elizabeth mumbled perfunctorily as she unscrewed the top of a bottle of Brights' President Burgundy. Susan hated cheap Brights' wine. It reminded her of those lonely sherry evenings after the divorce. "We might as well go into the living room," Elizabeth instructed. "I've ordered a pizza which Mike can pick up any time now."

The apartment felt painfully familiar to Susan. The kitchen tiles were still chipped. On the mantel was the garish oil painting done by Elizabeth's brother before his electric shock therapy. The metal floor lamp was still missing the middle button.

Mike stuck his head in the living room. "Is the pizza ready?"

"More than," said Elizabeth.

"See you guys in ten minutes," he said, slamming the door behind him.

Susan wanted to explain that Mike had said it didn't matter when they arrived tonight. She also wanted to explain to Elizabeth that their affair three years before had been *his* idea. But she kept her silence now, as she had kept it then. Mike would have to break up his own marriage if that's what he wanted.

Susan ran her fingers over the nub of the corduroy cushion, remembering the hilarious day when they had filled the huge pillows, plagued by the sticky foam, looking like tar and feather victims.

"What happened to your pillows?" Elizabeth asked politely.

"I lent them to Erna before I left," Susan puzzled her memory. "She lent them to Harvey when they split up. He forgets who he lent them to!"

"I see Harvey once in a while. He's still working on his thesis about houses in Virginia Woolf."

"And when is *your* thesis going to be published?" Susan said.

"Spring, they say."

Mike flung open the front door. "It's still hot. I'll get some plates and be right in."

The smell of pepperoni filled the silent room. They each ate ravenously. Elizabeth went to the kitchen and brought back the Muscadet.

"Well, we certainly are quiet," Mike laughed. "I thought some honesty might clear the air. I had no idea it would leave it completely vacant."

Slowly, Susan sipped her wine. The delicacy of Muscadet

was lost in the cyclamate aftertaste of the Burgundy.

Mike leaned forward, "I know I'm grateful to Susan for coming back. It took courage. Besides," he turned to Elizabeth, "it's helped to settle some things between us."

"Or unsettle them," said Elizabeth.

"I didn't call to settle or unsettle anything," said Susan.

"So why did you call?" asked Elizabeth.

"She called because she loves us, both of us," Mike explained. "She wants to re-establish the tie."

"It's a pretty knotted tie," Elizabeth said.

Susan looked from one to the other, amazed, then angry. "Look, if you two want to fight, you don't need me."

Mike ignored her, reaching over for Elizabeth's hand. "Think of the risk she was taking. The humiliation. What if we had refused to see her?"

"Oh fuck the risk," said Elizabeth, knocking her wine on the rug. White wine, which wouldn't stain. "What kind of risk is it for her to come flying through town, just another stopover on her world adventure."

"If you want a world adventure," Mike said, "you can have a world adventure."

"Don't put her up as a model to me, mister. I'll bloody well pick my own models."

Possessed by sudden clarity, Susan said, "Why don't you have this argument after I leave. I'm not going to play Aunt Minerva from out of town catching all the flak. This sounds like an old fight, where I got off years ago."

Elizabeth looked at her, widening her eyes slightly, as if suddenly remembering their reconciliation in the Skylight Room last week.

"It's true," Elizabeth said, "that we only have a few hours until Susan's train leaves."

The wine helped. Anecdotes flowed as they reached the bottom of the Muscadet. More photo booth shots. Pictures of everyone candid. Posed. Overexposed. Libertarian to Marxist. Lapsed Catholic. Lesbian lovers. Marriage therapy. Camping holiday in the Durdoyne. The wine eased the purposefulness of the exchange. Did she know Harry was out of

the looney bin, working as a mail clerk? A certain draft resister had turned hippie autocrat. Glenn had come out at the
Gay Rights March. A too-tender friend was swallowed by bar-
biturates. Maybe they could take a holiday in California this
year? They would write, yes, as often as possible. Mike might
make it out to LA for a conference in May. They still planned
to have kids. In fact, Elizabeth thought her crazy mood this
week was due to her period being late; they had been trying
to get pregnant for a year. Susan poured herself another glass
to drown the jealousy with more gossip. Was that poet still
seducing ingénue reviewers? Did the Italian daughter next
door ever run away to the theatre?

By eleven o'clock, she almost regretted having to leave, but
she said, "The train goes soon. I really should call a cab."

"The phone is still in the bedroom," said Mike.

"At least we can make the call for her," Elizabeth said with
a strange urgency that sounded larger than hospitality.

Bedrooms aren't that painful, thought Susan, grateful that
she wasn't drunk enough to have said it aloud. She walked
briskly into the bedroom and picked up the telephone. Telephone book. Yellow pages, she thought hazily, lazily, and
dialed information.

"If the number you want is not in the directory, hang on
for a moment and an operator will answer." Rattle. Rattle.
"If the number you want is not in the directory. . . ." Rattle.
Rattle. "If the number. . . ." Rattle. Rattle.

Lyndon was shaking the bars of a cage while two larger mon-
monkeys sat back and stared. Three monkeys in a cage. She
was still sober enough to count.

A scream.

Her voice. The wine. The monkeys. She would not throw
up.

"Oh god, Susan, we should have told you," Elizabeth
rushed into the bedroom. "They frighten everybody. They
still scare me every once in a while. But Mike insists that we
keep them here. It's the warmest room."

Susan was silent.

Mike negotiated with the cab dispatcher. The two women

walked into the front room and sat on the cushions. Elizabeth took her hand.

"Oh, Susan, I wish we had more time. To ourselves."

Mike walked out, brushing his hands and trying not to laugh at the chaos. Susan stared at the corners of his involuntary smile, tempted herself to dissolve the whole evening in hilarity. However, she could not laugh. She could not cry. And she would not throw up.

"We both love you," Elizabeth said, holding Mike by one hand and Susan by the other.

Mike reached over and separated the drapes. The cab's headlights shot in like a flash bulb.

Susan kissed them each good-bye.

Mrs. Delaney's Dollar

"Quiet. The nice, quiet oriental waitress." That's how they ask for me. I do a good job, distinguishing between french fries and hashbrowns. Remembering the ketchup. Holding the mayonnaise.

"China doll," Mr. Pearson calls me, although I came from Kyoto at age twelve and my name on the peppermint plastic badge is three syllables too long for Chinese.

I try to ignore Mr. Pearson and wait on the silent man by the window. I've never seen this one before and am filled with relief. Maybe I'll never see him again. A drifter. You can tell by the way he slipped into the booth before I cleared the table, before I had a chance to pick up the dollar that Mrs. Delaney left me for her Golden Gate Breakfast, the eggs sunny side up. More sun than we'll see in San Francisco for a month.

Good girl. I am Mrs. Delaney's good girl even though she cannot be more than five years older. Even though she is an inch shorter than I, leprechauns being as tiny as China dolls.

So this silent man is in a hurry. Good, no chatter. The more people at my station, the more tips. One. Two. Three less days until retirement.

"Coffee," he murmurs, almost shyly, so that I like him. "And scrambled eggs with toast."

"Yes," I nod, giving him one of my few morning smiles. After noon, my mouth gets looser and I find it easier to smile. More tips then. I have practiced smiling in the morning, but it comes off as crooked and spoils my digestion so is not worth the gratuities. Speaking of which, where is Mrs. Delaney's dollar? Some days she is forgetful and returns to the café to deliver it straight into my hands, clucking about her "good girl," her "quiet one." Today I did see her leave it on the table before shuffling out the door. The silent man is trying not to notice me as I move the ashtray and the creamer in search of my money. He looks like he wishes he had brought a newspaper to read. Instead, he stares out at Market Street, peering through the rain for cosmic answers. He does not smell of meths or alcohol.

"My dollar," I say, to be precise about the amount and the ownership. "Have you seen my dollar?"

Stunned, he looks. Numb. He should try for
Hollywood this man. Maybe he is surprised I
speak English. I already know that he does.
"Coffee." He has betrayed his fluency. "Scrambled eggs."

"My tip," I say louder, loud enough to embar-
rass him in front of the other customers. But what
does he care? A drifter. That's the trouble with
drifters. Quick, easy turnover. But because they
are swift, they are often invisible in their coming
and going and taking.

"Have you seen my money?" I ask simply.

"No," he answers.

I have made it too simple.

Doris is eyeing me from the cash register. Get
a move on, she is thinking, can't you see I have a
line waiting here. Where's your engine, girl? I like
Doris. No nonsense.

So I file the orders with the chef and tell the
girls who are waiting for their plates what has happened. Hannah and Ethel look over at Mr. Drifter
and nod. Marlene says, "the bastard."

Marlene follows me back to the table. His
scrambled eggs are just cool enough to be unpleasant.
He will suffer in silence. Drifters aren't complainers.
Not Mr. Quiet Guys who meditate on the rain.
Thieves maybe. But never complainers.

"So you say it was a dollar, honey," asks Marlene in her loud Detroit voice. Twangy. She is
proud of that twang. She never says "Detroit." She
says "Motown."

"Yes," I say, setting the watery eggs on the table,
instead of in his lap where I would prefer to put
them. "Mrs. Delaney's usual tip."

"Well, it's got to be here somewhere, honey,"
says Marlene, louder than I have heard her talk even
when she was hailing the 38 Geary bus across two

lanes of traffic.

"'Scuse me," she says to the drifter. "But you didn't happen to see a dollar belonging to my friend here?"

"No," he says quietly into the soggy eggs, picking up a knife to butter the cold toast.

"Anybody around here seen a dollar?" Marlene asks. "Anybody seen Kimiko's tip?"

Startled faces. Shaking heads. A few appropriately critical glances to the man slowly eating his cold eggs.

Other work to do. You don't wait around all morning for a dollar even if you can't spare a smile until noon.

I am delivering three orders of Blueberry Mountain Pancakes when I notice Hannah and Ethel running the carpet sweeper. What are they doing? We never sweep 'till after closing. Even then, it's not the waitresses. The union would never stand for it. Whatever they're doing, I hope Doris, who is the union steward, doesn't catch them. I've had enough bad feelings today.

"Sir, could you move your feet?" says Hannah.

"Must be around here somewhere," says Ethel. "Haven't seen a dollar, have you?"

He is beginning the last quarter of toast. Without removing his mouth from the slice, he shakes his head. Suddenly I notice how tired he looks, lost.

"Hey, China doll," calls Mr. Pearson. "How about a little more coffee, quiet one."

I pour the coffee and move quickly from Mr. Pearson before he can touch me. Quiet one! I think of the silent screams of Hiroshima every time they say "quiet one." I'm so eager to escape that I find myself going to fill the thief's cup. He regards me through astonished, bloodshot eyes and says, "Thank you."

The blueberry pancakes need more butter and Mr. Pearson thinks he'll have a second donut after all.

By the time I turn around, Mr. Drifter has vanished. Julio has cleaned the table. In the ashtray is Mrs. Delaney's dollar. And beneath it, a shiny silver dollar. And beneath that, a note. "How lucky I was to get the quiet one."

XI

Side/Stroke

Her head was still swimming from the wine and her race to the station as the train pulled through shadows of Toronto rowhouses. Susan sat back in her compartment, watching the moon flood Lake Ontario. She was filled with tears. In mourning. She was leaving herself behind and going home. Leaving friends in England and Canada to see if she were still an American. Crazy really, after six years away. Only one more year was needed. All the cells in your body change every seven years.

She tried to concentrate on the book. Horrible scene about a dog-cat. Terrible book, *Memoirs of a Survivor.* Cheap fantasia. Why hadn't she stopped with *The Summer Before The Dark?* Susan never thought this would happen; she had run out of Lessing to read. She took a long drink of wine.

◇

Another glass of red wine. Thick, black Ontario sky with silver spurs. Pretzels.

Susan was in the bar car now with a dozen other midnight travellers. The couple to one side was playing pinochle.

"I'm not mourning Canada or England," she heard herself saying, "so much as I'm mourning the woman I was six years ago." Susan was talking to an older woman—probably fifty or fifty-five—and a man in his thirties. The man ordered a bottle of burgundy.

"I miss that idealism," Susan said, "that basic morality."

145

Why was she rambling on to these strangers. Maybe what you said when travelling didn't count. Promises, confessions, secrets—they would all disappear at the time of arrival.

"In the days when I left the States," she continued, "I was young enough to take risks."

"Well, you had faith," said the older woman.

"People don't use words like 'faith' nowadays," smiled Susan.

He laughed. "Or words like 'nowadays.' You two sound like frontier moralists. Makes me feel ancient."

"Sometimes I like feeling ancient," reflected Susan.

She poured herself another glass of wine. She was looking forward to California and the good, cheap wine. She never drank much when she lived there. Maybe that's one of the reasons she had had to leave.

◊

The next morning they all met in the breakfast car at the edge of the Prairies. Funny how you set yourself up when you travel, thought Susan. You check out people for politics, education, style, like choosing partners across a dance floor. The talk came easily after the coffee was poured.

Susan remembered now: Adam was a lawyer going to a consumer rights conference in Vancouver. He was very like Guy in some ways, except for the blond hair. A nice man, actually. The woman was immediately sympathetic. Sara Gold: Jewish mother: a professor of English in Victoria. Her fingers were heavily ringed in turquoise, silver and ivory. No wedding band. Susan always wondered how women of that generation had survived without wedding bands.

"You can go back and reread the other Lessing books," Sara suggested. Susan acknowledged that she often returned to *The Golden Notebook* for solace. Adam said he liked *Briefing For A Descent Into Hell* the best.

"My wife was really into Lessing just before the divorce," he said. "I read her to see what was happening between us."

"And did you find out?" asked Sara.

"I found out that it wasn't Lessing that was between us," he smiled.

Susan nodded kindly. She liked him. She was glad she no longer felt responsibility as a feminist for every divorce in town.

They talked into the late morning, until the land was so flat that you could see everywhere and nowhere at once. They would stop in Winnipeg for an hour-and-a-half. Sara suggested that they all get off the train and eat lunch at the Prince George.

Susan was disappointed. She liked eating on the train. It reassured her that travelling was a normal way of life. But she also liked Adam and Sara. They had relieved her of those usual travelling jitters—of shyness, boredom, anger at being stuck in inane conversations about West End London shows or about how we really watch too much TV or about World War II in St. Louis. She was enjoying their company.

In fact, she liked *him* a lot. An affair would be safe. After two nights, they would split for opposite ends of the coast. He was bright, too much of a fuzzy liberal, but funny. Did Sara disapprove of her flirting? Maybe Susan just imagined it.

Winnipeg was clear and warm. "There are always three or four crystal days like this in the fall," according to Sara. "But I look forward to winter, to the security of warmth under the snow."

After lunch, they returned to their separate compartments. Susan returned to her journal. "What a year to come back," she wrote. "Bicentennial year. Good god. I have no class." She had read *Burr* to put an ironic lease on things, but the book had just made her angrier. Vidal's aristocratic distance outraged her. She really wished she were more dispassionate, or at least that she could see things from the sidelines once in a while. That's what living abroad had meant to her. Being on the sidelines. Life didn't seem to count as much in Canada or England. As an expatriate, she could make mistakes and not fail; she could fail and not sink.

But of course that's why she decided to come back. Nothing seemed quite real while she was away. Like the abortion march from Charing Cross to Hyde Park. She had watched her flatmates up there in doctors' uniforms and Pia running around with her camera and Carol leading the "Free Abortion on Demand" chants. The demonstration was important. She was with her friends. But somehow, it seemed more *real* to her that women couldn't get abortions in New Jersey. She had had the same problem when she lived in Canada. As an ardent Canadian nationalist, she continued to subscribe to *The Nation* and wanted the books she wrote to be available in Cody's on Telegraph Avenue. American was the only skin that seemed to fit. You have to go home again.

"At least for a visit," she was telling Adam later that afternoon.

"How come you haven't gone back before now?"

"Because of the war."

"But you weren't a draft dodger," he laughed nervously, running his hand through that blond hair.

"There were more of us than you think," she answered. "Anyway, I didn't feel it was fair to go back until Guy, my husband, was 'pardoned.' "

"Do you feel absolved?" he asked.

"Absolved by Guy, in a small way."

Time for a game of pinochle before the second sitting of dinner. Susan rested on the countryside, occasionally turning to watch Sara and Adam play. Sara's ringed hands, strong and competent versus Adam's freckled fingers, quick and keen. He would be good in bed. Outside there was more bush now. She felt easier, escaping the Prairies, approaching the West where trees and mountains and beaches were large enough, scaled to life. Now, if she could only slip below the border without drowning.

The funny Australian with the *Motorcycle Maintenance* magazine had sat down across from them at dinner.

"Rhyming slang," he prattled. "Ain't you never heard of it? I say 'china plate,' and I mean 'mate.' It's Aussie rhyming slang."

He proceeded to entertain them with tales of the travels he

148

was making on a legacy from his grandfather. Susan tried talking with him about Britain, which he didn't like because it was too old. Now he was headed for Tierra del Fuego.

"It's cold down there," said Sara.

"Yeah, the end of the earth. You been?"

"Yes," said Sara mysteriously, "but not on a motorcycle."

Susan didn't catch any more. Adam was asking why she left England.

"Because of the cold." She told him about writing in her flat, listening to a friend's abandoned *California Dreaming* album, scared that she was going to be asphixiated by the faulty gas heater. Waiting forty minutes for the Northern Line in the sooty draught of tube stations. Working at the Cooperative Press where wind seeped through the plexiglass. After a while, her romance had turned to self-pity. The tea kettle in her flat stopped whistling; she could never quite get it up to boiling again. The inflated pound was falling into the Common Market. She was too guilty to feel uncomfortable. Then she became too sick to feel anything at all. When Susan left England, she willed the Feliciano album to her friend Pia who stayed behind.

Adam looked at her like she was Margaret Sanger. Susan found a familiar pleasure in this admiration. Sara, who had been listening silently, smiled over everyone and suggested they order another bottle of Cabernet to keep them warm. Was Sara pushing her together with Adam or was Susan imagining it? Adam talked about Margaret Atwood's sense of the Canadian aesthetic in *Survival.* An interesting discussion, Susan thought, so why did Sara turn back to the Australian?

Everyone was a bit tipsy as they climbed the stairs to the Vista Dome. There were no booths for four—only two small tables at opposite ends of the car. Susan wanted to talk more with Sara, realized that they had been apart all day, since lunch. But it seemed natural for them to split into dinner partners. She and Adam here; Sara and the Australian at the far end of the car.

Clearly, Adam liked her. He talked avidly about his last visit to the States. He told her he liked her. He held her hand.

149

Gently, she retrieved it to sip her Kahlua Alphonse.

Susan could hear her laughter from the other end of the car. Sara's head was flung back so far that you could just see the tip of her chin. That's what Susan wanted—simply to have a good time, to relax, to get out of herself. Fucking was too complicated. The Kahlua was getting to her. It was either alcohol or the damn sugar. Susan was neither a romantic nor a prude, but sometimes these mating rituals got so gross. Goodnight, she said, rather surprising both of them.

◇

The next morning, she woke to mountains. This was like being in a pup tent with a window, only better because you were moving. She remembered how much she had drank the the previous evening and waited for the hang-over, but it did not come. She lay with her head in the trees, daydreaming of snow. Maybe she would skip breakfast. Who would notice? The friendship had been broken last night. And she wasn't very hungry.

Sara sat across the table from Adam. The Australian was nowhere around.

"I don't know what happened to him," said Sara. "He was on his ninth Guinness when I tottered off to bed."

"He and I stayed up to 3:00 a.m. making rhymes," Adam grinned. "See, you women can't hold your liquor."

Maybe he wasn't too angry, Susan thought. Maybe they *would* make love tonight.

"So what will you do when you get to California?" asked Sara.

"Find out if I'm an American," answered Susan. "I'm not sure what it means anymore."

"Sounds grand," said Adam.

"It *is* grand," said Sara.

Sara told them that she came home to British Columbia every year after a month's holiday in Quebec. Life wouldn't be worth living without Quebec, but she would have nothing to live on there. Drawn to the melancholy in Sara's voice, Susan was disappointed that she and Adam had consumed so much conversation with their inexperience. Sara told them now about nursing in China during the Long March, about bringing a Quebec amputee back to Montreal and marrying him. They had become young Reds in the fifties. They met the RCMP on Mont Royal. And Sara was faced with an unrenewed contract at the university, a divorce, no place to go but home to British Columbia. B.C. needed professors and they never heard about things as far away as Quebec demonstrations. She had settled into a grey clapboard house by the ocean with a woman friend for a while, and now alone.

While Adam played solitaire, Susan and Sara sipped tea in the Vista Dome, floating together under the sequoias and swapping other journeys.

Susan, all by herself at fourteen, took the Union Pacific from San Francisco to Seattle to visit her girlfriends.

Sara had taken the Trans-Siberian Railway and it arrived in Vladivostok on time.

The Tan-Zam Railway got to Dar es Salaam one minute early, said Susan.

These were the same cups Sara had used on the CNR during the war.

The first time Susan had understood what "bloody cold" meant was when she and Guy took that train to Hudson Bay.

"Snowing outside," Adam's voice carried across the car. "It will be snowing when we stop at Jasper."

Sara remembered that the train between Montreal and Quebec City was a very long journey in 1956.

Susan's train from Moscow to Prague was scheduled for August 22. The Soviet troops got there first. She flew to Vienna, instead, August 22, 1968.

◇

The stopover in Jasper took an hour. Sara linked Susan's arm at the sheepskin elbow. Susan took Adam's arm. They shot photos by the bear statue and then walked around the village eating hot french fries. The Australian anxiously badgered a porter to let him check on his motorcycle which had never been exposed to such fucking cold in its life. Sorry man, said the West Indian guard, no one could enter the freight car. And if *he*, from Jamaica for god's sake, could cope with the cold, so could a motorcycle. Susan suggested that they warm themselves up. The four of them, holding hands, ran around the train together.

Susan went back to her journal, wrote a few lines and watched the snowflakes leafing from bare trees. She thought about trains passing from Warsaw to Oaxaca to Penzance. "When Lilacs Last in the Dooryard Bloomed." Mombassa to Nairobi to Chartres. And now she was going home. She had never really learned another language properly. She wrote only American. She was going home on her own. For the past six years she had lived by maps. She wouldn't need maps at home. One got on by instinct, by some kind of genetic survival code. She was going back to save her own life.

Adam dropped by the compartment with a yellow rose.

"I bought it in Jasper," he explained. "When you two were in the ladies' room."

So much for lifesaving instructions. She joined him for a recess in the Vista Dome.

Late that afternoon, Susan heard Sara's bracelets jangling behind her and turned into a warm wave of Chanel 19.

"Sleep well, my dear?" she asked Sara, a little surprised with her own familiarity.

"Wonderfully," said Sara. "I dreamt I was riding on a train for the rest of my life."

The Australian surfaced at dinner and invited them all to his compartment for cognac afterwards. Apparently grandpa believed in lubricating the ride. It was a cozy room with everything necessary, and a few things unnecessary. A miniature apartment. They talked about different dollhouses they had each inhabited—in other train compartments, boat cabins, Volkswagon busses.

Susan leaned back against Adam's hand. He moved the strap of her dress back and forth. Back and forth.

Sara was telling them about the old days on the Orient Express—about a trip she took to Bucharest with her lover Pat before the war. "Velvet cushions, porcelain bowls," she recalled. "Tea and croissants for breakfast."

Rubbing her foot along Adam's herringboned calf, Susan was lulled by Sara's voice and the cognac. You learned so much travelling, she thought mistily, but the only moving she wanted to do now was into Adam's compartment. Perhaps she could just excuse herself and he would discreetly follow.

"What I remember best about that trip was Virginia Woolf," said Sara. *Three Guineas* and *To The Lighthouse.* Since then, I've always taken her on train journeys. Just finished *A Room Of One's Own* again today."

Susan caught herself staring at Sara. She felt a little dazed by the drink. By Sara's ice blue eyes. Cognac on the rocks.

"I've always wanted to read that one," Susan said. "The novels intimidate me in their languor, but I've heard that book is wonderful."

Adam was arguing with the Australian, declaring hockey absolutely more violent than soccer. Susan leaned forward and listened to Sara talking about Woolf with the same intensity she felt for Lessing. How nice to see Sara with her guard down, her spirit up. Susan felt a sudden closeness to her, a merging.

"Come," said Sara. "Before we part tomorrow morning, I'd like to give you Virginia Woolf as a farewell present."

"Actually, I was thinking about going to bed pretty soon," Susan said. "Or I'll be in no shape tomorrow for the Greyhound to California." Adam's eyes were lost to cognac. There was no hope, no worry, about being followed.

As they walked between the cars, the night air hit Susan like sleet. Nervous about the border tomorrow, she felt chilled, then sweaty. How she could die of her own fever sometimes.

"Come in," said Sara. "I'll find it in a minute." Susan sat on the bed which the porter had unlatched. Cold, ironed sheets. Hotel. Hospital. Prison. Train. Heavy, sanitized wool blankets. Warm, functionally warm.

"I'm always freezing in these compartments," said Sara.

"How about you?"

She nodded and Sara handed her a very worn Fairisle sweater. Susan was glad to stay and talk, to postpone tomorrow. She liked the Chanel 19 and Sara's own scent that the sweater bore around her.

"Isn't it grand—the trees and these mountains," said Sara, looking out the window. "Such elegant strength."

Susan agreed. "I'm relieved to be back West. I got so weary of sweet English countryside. Once we crossed that first ledge of mountains today, I felt we were back in the land of the possible."

"You do have a young, fresh optimism."

"Not so young," said Susan.

Sara put her hand on Susan's shoulder. "You misunderstand. I value that. I covet it."

Susan turned to her. "If you only knew how much I admired your grace and . . . discipline," she stammered. Damn. It was up to Sara to reach out now.

"We can have both," Sara answered vaguely.

Susan smelled the anger in her own sweat. Anger at the cool academic distance between them. She hated Sara who could see her fever. She loved Sara, loved the fantasy of the two of them in a grey clapboard house by the ocean. She could stay in Canada; she could be loved and held here on the edge.

Sara kissed her. She held Susan firmly, but lightly. Susan had not felt real tenderness since Pia. Aching with the need for this warmth, she reached for Sara's breasts. Would they be fat or flaccid? Who knows how a woman weathers fifty years? Full, firm whiteness poured into the stiff red nipples.

Sara's cool strength had gone to hunger. Sensing the change, Susan was moved and frightened.

"Will you stay with me?" Sara whispered.

"How long?" Susan wanted to ask, but instead she pulled off her dress and slid between the cold white sheets wondering if goose bumps on her flesh would make her more sexy. She watched Sara drop the long, woven skirt from her waist. Her bottom was round, full. Her legs were sturdy. She longed for

Sara's experience and at the same time worried that she could not satisfy the older woman. Sara seemed to know what she wanted, running her hands softly over Susan's breasts and stomach, licking and sipping from her vagina, circling and tapping with her tongue, licking and sipping. Then she moved Susan's hands over her own body with gentle encouragement. Gentleness. Susan couldn't remember such gentleness even from childhood. Rocking each other, stroking each other. The child is mother of the woman. Rocking with the train. First class compartment from Brighton to London, tired after a Sunday on the beach. Slow, hollow coach from Amoy to Hong Kong, with Japanese POW's silent in their healed wounds. The sleeper to Edinburgh. The commute to Manchester. Toronto to Chicago to Shanghai to Montreal to Victoria to San Francisco to Antigua to Canterbury to Maputo to Vancouver.

Susan woke from a jolt of the train and felt that Sara's arms were still around her. Still. Perfect stillness. She worried that the motionlessness might waken Sara, might disconnect them. They turned together, Susan making a cave around Sara's body. The train began to move again. Susan fell back to sleep.

"First call for breakfast," a harsh disembodied voice. "Vancouver in an hour-and-a-half."

Sara's arms held her as they crossed the Frazer Canyon. Susan turned to Sara's open eyes. They kissed.

◇

Sara said she could postpone Victoria for a few days. Would Susan like to stay in Vancouver together? Of course Susan wanted to stay, to rest safely here above the border. But she told Sara that she had to catch a Greyhound for the States today. Maybe Sara could come down to California for a visit?

Whistles. Squeaking wheels. Baggage calls. "Vancouver in five minutes."

"Will you write to me Sara?"

"Will you write about me, Susan?"

Rain railed as the train skidded into Vancouver. They lost each other in the shuffle for bags and coats and tickets. Susan tried to find Sara outside the station. But everyone was turtled under black umbrellas. At the corner, Susan hailed a cab for the Greyhound depot. It was pouring so hard, she might have drowned just waiting for the light to change.

Well Past the Weird Hour

It was well past the weird hour, she thought, as she rode the escalator down to the BART platform. She hadn't always been this paranoid. No, the word was "cautious." Then her friend Clara was beaten and raped. Indeed, a woman couldn't be too cautious nowadays. She watched a delicate man with purple punk hair running his hand along a pointed object in his back pocket. Three jiving boys heckled all the girls as they walked by the car. A strange old lady carrying two Macy's shopping bags, Christmas 1976, was mumbling angrily. Well past the weird hour, all right. She spotted a dumpy kid studying the jackets of two classical LP's. He looked pretty innocuous. She squeezed near him.

"Hey, who are you pushing around?" said a mean-looking woman in a cowboy hat.

"Oh, excuse me, I didn't notice."

"Fuck that," said the cowboy hat. "Back of the line, babe."

He was pretty dumpy looking. Probably no one else would want to sit next to him anyway. A safe refuge from all points of view.

She was right. There he sat crumpled next to the window, reading the liner on his Bach cantatas. She felt sorry for him, so lonely looking. Sometimes San Francisco did seem like a big city. She pulled out a copy of *Time* and turned to the movie reviews.

"Do you live in San Francisco?"

She looked around. The boys were snickering to themselves. The old woman was slumped in the front seat, humming. It was him, Mr. Crumple.

She nodded—no reason to be nervous she told herself—and turned the page.

"What part?" he asked like he was making wedding reception conversation.

"Sixteenth " she lied, hoping he would get off the train before her stop on twenty-fourth.

"What street?"

She gave him a long look—which neither discouraged him nor gave her any clues about his intentions. He still looked like the honest schmuck she saw at the BART station.

"Sanchez," she said, recalling the street where her boyfriend of twenty years ago, a quarterback, had lived.

"Oh, that's nice," he said, adjusting the plastic satchel on his lap. She realized that he probably had a sawed-off shotgun in there. Come to think of it, he did look a little weird. Maybe he was one of those XXY chromosome types.

He was silent. She returned to the article on pornography.

"You have a New York accent," he said.

She nodded.

"Do you mind if I ask what part you're from?"

"Near Houston Street," she said, sensing that he was also Lower Eastside Irish.

"Me too," he said. "Did you go to St. Mike's?"

"Yeah." She wondered if he were Tommy Dunnigan grown up or Bobby Driscoll, those creeps who used to beat up her little brother George. "Did you go to St. Mike's too?" she asked.

"No," he said.

She looked around, but saw no other free seats. And no old people standing. The train was only halfway through the tunnel. What if he pulled something right here in the tunnel?

"You like it in California?" he asked.

"It's OK," she said.

"How long have you lived here?"

"Twenty-five years," she said, in a louder voice, hoping to attract attention to them just in case. That punk rock guy looked like he could take care of Mr. Crumple if he wanted. Lord, she was always such a bad judge of character.

"Do you work in the city?"

"Yes," she said. She fancied telling him she was a ballistics expert in the San Francisco Police Department. But even joking, she couldn't call herself a cop.

"I'm just here on vacation," he said.

"Having a nice time?" she said, in spite of herself.

"Oh, my, yes," he said. "And I find you Californians so friendly." He stood up. "Well, this is my stop. Thanks for the conversation."

She watched him get off the train and walk to the escalator, confused, and weighed down by his airline satchel and his classical records. What kind of world was it where a big strong woman like herself was afraid of a little Mr. Crumple? She looked around to see the kids at the back of the car smoking and yelling to the fancy girls carrying opera programs. The punk man was engrossed in his fanzine, running a blue comb through his purple locks. The old woman had her head on her bosom, snoring.

XII

Novena

It all came back to Susan like the rosaries, one decade after another. First her mother Mary's story and then Susan's own story. Sometimes Susan confused the two stories, in the sense that we are all each other's memories and premonitions.

Mary

Pubic hair, dark curls against blue white skin, is all she remembered of her own mother. Mary was seven-and-a-half when the "doctor" left her mother dead on the kitchen table. They said her mother was a blonde, but Mary didn't remember. They said her mother was French. Mary appreciated that when she was older. (Stuart romance in Edinburgh's dour back streets.) The pubic hair, she did remember, was flecked with grey.

Susan

The blood on the sheets of the double bed came from her toes, Susan's mother said. From clipping her toenails too close. But it smelled of sex and she couldn't fool Susan with this fairy tale. Susan was already eight, so she knew she was too old to be an orphan and she remembered more than pubic hair. Susan remembered that when her father was at sea and her mother slept alone, there was blood on the ironed muslin sheets. She would crawl in next to Mom, snuggling away from the nightmares. Her mother never revealed her own dark dreams. But Susan knew, even then, that the blood was too high up for toes.

Mary

Mary's mother's photograph stood on the bookcase for four years after her death. Later, Mary could never remember her mother's face, but she did remember all the books, each by place. Fifty years later. The Everyman volumes of Scott, the red leather Burns. And the Milton. Mary's father would bring down *Paradise Lost* and read her the order of the world. He would leave her oatmeal bubbling on the stove each morning. Mary always came straight home from school and prepared his supper. They took care of each other this way after her mother's death. But there was never enough warmth for his cough.

Susan

Susan's grandma, her father's mother, lived in the upstairs bedroom and never cried. Sometimes the "Jesus, Mary and Joseph" under her breath was more expletive than prayer, but Susan never saw the tears. Urine bottle on the lace doily. "Would you empty it dear?" Susan pretended it was orange juice and never smelled the difference. She took care of her father's mother the way she would have taken care of her father if he had ever been home. Yellow pus oozed from her grandma's leg ulcer as Susan changed the muslin dressings. She washed yesterday's blood from these remnants. They dried outside on the line, slightly yellower than the double bed sheets, the stains gone from both. Susan never heard her mother *or* her grandma cry. Not even over onions.

Mary

Mary bawled with anger. On a sunny Saturday morning riding the Princes Street trolley down toward Leith and Portabello Beach. She was going home alone from the Royal Infirmary. When they had registered the night before, him alternately choking and spitting blood, he told her not to worry. God would take care of them both. He reminded Mary that HE would always be with her. And these people on the trolley, what right did they have to live, to laugh? She would never forget him, never. He would always be with her.

Susan

He came back periodically. Susan didn't remember much about her father, but she did remember the Japanese stamps, the Easter cablegram and a telephone call from Argentina just to say hello. Her mother polished the Swiss music box, dusted the ivory elephant carvings from India and the fat ceramic god Ho Tai. Susan remembered her mother being happy for days before he returned. Once he brought back three bronze busts, of women in the traditional coiffures of Cambodia, Laos and Vietnam, cut off just before the nipples. He would stay home for two or three months at a time.

Mary

Broken chocolate and the *News of the World*. Mary would run down Leith Walk for their treats and race back home for the two evening hours before the coal fire. Her little brother Peter was there, too. Beautiful, blond Peter. (It must have been true about her mother being a French blonde.) But *she* was his daughter. "Remember you're a Gibson and I love you," her father would say. She knew that, even the day he chased her out of St. Mary's Cathedral with a switch. All right to play with Maria Ciotti, to eat her mother's spaghetti, but never let him catch her again in that Papist sanctuary. She remembered for a long time afterward because the switching was so unlike him.

Susan

Susan's mother taught her the Hail Mary, the Our Father, the Glory Be. Susan brought home the classroom rosary beads in the belly of the statue of the Infant of Prague which opened at the bottom like a piggy bank. Sister Matthew told them that the family that prays together stays together. But one afternoon when Susan was sitting with her father watching the Dodgers smash the Giants, he told her that her mother wasn't Catholic. She screamed and demanded he tell her she wasn't Jewish. (Sister Matthew had warned about the Jews.) "Go ask your mother," he teased, "go tell her you thought she was a Jew." "Protestant," Mary said heavily. She put her arms around Susan and told her God loved everyone. But Susan knew, then, that her mother Mary would not be saved.

Mary

After his death, Mary's half sisters were always around—like faded aunts, somewhere in the background. They were kind to her but restrained. Their mother, who was her mother, had run away to live with her father, who was not their father. Jennie, Kate, Patsy were older sisters who treated her kindly, especially after everyone's mother died. Mary. She was sweet, wee Mary. But neither Mary nor her sisters could forget she was a Gibson.

Susan

When Susan told Ann Crisillo that her family was moving all the way to Seattle for her father's shore job, Ann let Susan into the clique. Susan was invited to play in the family room which Dr. Crisillo had panelled and hung with the heads of dead animals. There was an all-color gumball machine. In June, Ann Crisillo came around to the house and pressed her nose on the warm back door screen. "Mrs. Campbell, will you see Eskimos in Seattle?" Susan was mortified by the question. She dreaded her mother's honest, boring answer. "There are snowy mountains," said her mother, "and the Pacific Ocean." The Pacific Ocean! Ann and Susan regarded each other seriously. They were passionate friends those last three weeks in New Jersey on the Atlantic Ocean.

Mary

Now, Mary always thought of her favorite teacher, Miss Mackie, when she started her shift at Fairley's Café. It was a kind of magic insurance policy against Miss Mackie coming in and discovering that she wasn't going to be a bookkeeper after all. That day, two years before, when Miss Mackie treated her to lunch at Fairley's had been the high point of Mary's entire life. Better than being Top Student. Better than getting married which Mary would never do anyway because she was going to be a career woman like Miss Mackie, as she had promised her father.

Susan

Susan's chubby thighs stuck to the green naugahyde chair. She cried and cried. The kitchen chair had been baking on the sidewalk with the rest of the furniture, ready to be confiscated by the Mayflower man. It took a while for them to find her bawling in the street. "Some sight you make, clownface," her mother said. "I won't go." "He'll always be with us from here on out," her mother said. "I won't go." Her mother hugged her tightly. Susan didn't want to be childish, so she went into her empty bedroom and played with the doll Ann Crisillo gave her to make them blood sisters. The doll's arms fell off just before supper.

Mary

Mary saw them come in the side door. Miss Mackie and a pudgy little girl smiling and chattering under her freckles and straw hat and red hair. Luckily, Mary's morning shift was almost over. She had a date with that sailor Andy Campbell who always wanted her to marry him and go off to America.

Susan

It was late. Susan's father never came home before midnight now. Because of this Alaska oil line. Tricky business. So Susan would sit up with her mother and talk about times as long ago as Ann Crisillo and the Eskimos. Susan always fell asleep in algebra the next morning, but someone had to stay up with her mother to say he would be all right. Even though the roads were slippery and he was a terrible driver, especially through whiskey fumes. Susan longed for the Easter cablegrams and the calls from Argentina. She knew it would never be all right and here they were on the edge of the Pacific Ocean. Susan wished he would die. Instead, he and the bleach-blonde woman took off together for San Diego.

◇

Grey hair across the booth of the downtown diner. Mary's hazel eyes reflecting back to Susan what once was, what might have been. She cuts the deck, deals them each a canasta hand and keeps an eye out for customers. An old lady, cashiering at an all-night coffee shop. A middle-aged daughter, keeping her company. Hail Mary. Our Father. Glory Be. The words slip out with the cards. Who said them? Neither woman acknowledges. But perhaps someday yet they will talk about the blood too high up for toes.

The Green Loudspeaker

The green loudspeaker was the first thing Emily noticed about school. The round, peeling, chartreuse loudspeaker hung over the Ten Commandments which hung over the blackboard. Every morning class commenced with a voice from the loudspeaker—Sister Mary Francis calling them to their feet to pledge allegiance to the flag (to God and our country) and to pray the Our Father. They would all look up at the box—as if waiting for Howdy Doody to appear—and listen to the announcements about confession schedule, lunch milk duty, and the competition to adopt Pagan Babies.

After that, the perforated green box was silent until the next morning, unless. Unless, and Emily's heart beat faster thinking of this, unless Sister Mary Francis had to call someone to her office on "a discipline issue." Barbara Francini was called twice in the first grade, once for shooting a water pistol and once for not wearing underpants. Barbara was the kind of tough girl Emily's mother had told her to avoid. The near occasion of sin Father Boyle had warned about. Barbara would grow into one of those juvenile delinquents they described in *Look Magazine*.

Emily's older brother Tommy had been called up at least once a term for fights at recess or for insolence to his teachers. By the eighth grade Tommy was a veteran. He was tough, but not delinquent material. He was too busy playing baseball, practicing to make the Majors like their father never had. Tommy didn't mind being called up. He always laughed about it after school. But Emily was worried, worried for his immortal soul if he kept on disobeying like that. Everytime she heard Sister Mary Francis call "Tommy Dolan" over the loudspeaker, she worried. She had the fear of God in her, that girl, and the fear of Sister Mary Francis.

Sometimes she tried to think of the loudspeaker as the Wizard of Oz. She would stare at the zillion holes in the round circle and imagine magic. Actually, she knew how it worked. She found out one morning when she had been excused from class with a sudden case of diarrhea. Quickly she rushed through the empty corridor, the voice of Sister Mary Francis echoing from the open classroom doors. Passing the glass-enclosed principal's office, she saw the old nun (forty at least, according to Mama) leaning over the microphone and reading the novena schedule from a long yellow pad. She scurried by lest Sister catch her and demand an explanation that would be heard over the loudspeaker. Sister Mary Francis wasn't the sort to get diarrhea, especially not before class had even started.

Emily survived almost four years of Assumption School without being summoned by the loudspeaker. Then one afternoon during geography class, in the middle of a confusing discussion about isthmuses and peninsulas, she heard the loud click. Like the click of her parents' alarm clock which woke her before the bell woke them. "An isthmus is," she repeated to herself, concentrating, trying not to worry about the imminent voice of Sister Mary Francis, just as at home she would try not to waken from the alarm's click and worry about the day ahead.

"Good afternoon," came the cool, crisp voice. "Good afternoon students and teachers."

Emily knew that today she would not understand isthmuses.

"Will the following students please come to my office immediately: "Emily Dolan. . . ."

She did not hear the other names. Accomplices? All she could hear was "Emily Dolan." "Emily Dolan." "Dolan," with a tint of Irish like Grandma Helen. Emily Dolan. Cool, clear. No doubt she was being called. Is this what a vocation was like? Would the call be this clear? Of course she always knew it would happen. Always knew she would be found out. And so it was with some excitement and fear that Emily got to her feet, walked past Sister Mary William, whose face betrayed only the slightest distraction from her geography glossary, past the desk of Barbara Francini, whose eyes showed a new respect for Emily. Nervous, yet

prepared to face the will of God, Emily walked
into the hallway. She noticed how the waxed
floor shone yellow from the flourescent ceiling
lamps.

Half-an-hour later, Emily quietly slipped into
her desk. Sister Mary William faced the blackboard
and did not even glance up from the long division
with which she, herself, was having some trouble.
Emily pulled out her exercise pad and flew through
math like she had never flown before. Every once
in a while, her hand would brush against the bulge
in her sweater pocket and she would glance at the
loudspeaker in the same complicity she felt with
certain statues in church.

Not until 2:45 did Sister Mary William notice
her sitting there. She assigned a short writing
exercise and called Emily to her desk to inquire
about the summons. The nun blushed and looked
like she might cry as Emily returned to her place.

"Class," Sister cleared her throat. "I have an
announcement to make."

Emily tried to keep her eyes off the loudspeaker.

"Sister Mary Francis has just awarded Emily the
4th grade literary prize for her poem, 'Jesus' Love
at Easter.' "

Emily could hear Barbara Francini's short,
gruff laugh. A few 'oohs' and 'ahhs.' But most
of the other kids could have cared less since it
was five past three and they wanted class dismissed.

Tommy waited for Emily after school like he
hadn't waited since she was in kindergarten and he
was required to walk his sister home.

"So whadid they send ya up for?" he asked, re-
vealing both pride and astonishment. "My baby
sister and old Battleaxe Francis. Whadid they get
ya for?"

Emily looked at him, past him and saw through his toughness, saw through Barbara Francini's smirk.

"Gone deaf?" asked Tommy, pronouncing it "deef" like he had heard on *Gunsmoke.* "I said, whadid they get you for?"

"They got me for a poem," she said.

"A what?" He started to laugh.

But she was already three paces ahead.

XIII
Afterlife

"I've got to get back to work."

"Judy will be hurt if you go."

"Ridiculous. With twenty other people here, she doesn't have time to talk with me. Besides, she's tucked in the corner with that Englishman."

"Then there's Hank. Remember how hard it was to approach a writer when you were in school?"

"Oh, fuck Hank. I've got my own work to do."

Susan tried to stop bickering with herself and examined the Guatemalan tapestry on the opposite wall. She wished Hank would hurry up with that cheese and wine. She hoped he would remember "dry"; she couldn't handle a hangover tomorrow.

Too much work. What to do while she waited? She was over thirty years old and still nervous about being spotted alone at a party, still self-conscious enough to try to look busy studying album covers and tapestries. Really, she did have better uses for her time. Like the book. Oh, it had become an obsession. Her friends had learned to treat it like a difficult child—or treat her like a difficult parent—inquiring tentatively, offering generous, but puzzled sympathy.

Susan left the party quickly, not bothering to take Judy away from the Englishman or Hank away from the gobs of sweaty cheese. They would understand.

(*"A writer, you know, actually makes her living by it. Maybe a little shy, eccentric, maybe even a little neurotic about her work, but in a productive way."*)

Lately Susan often left places in the middle of the evening to go back to her office. She was finding social life, these civil banalities, anecdotes, pickups, such a waste of time. Now she was always calculating time, always looking downhill—only three more days until Friday; only two more hours until bed. Parties and leisurely lunches and midnight telephone conversations all seemed so extraneous, such a waste of time. They interrupted work or postponed sleep. How had she spent so many hours just lying around listening to her clock radio when she was fourteen or talking to Guy in their tiny kitchen in Toronto when they were first married? How was there more time then?

The street lamps along Hearst Avenue condensed the cold night into stalactites of potential energy. She watched the cars cut through luminous fog, sliding toward the bridge to San Francisco. San Francisco. Her father had worked from all those port towns to be stationed one day in San Francisco. San Francisco was why she moved from school to school. Eventually the family wound up in a suburb, city rents being what they were, of San Francisco. San Francisco of Oriental steamers, gold rushes, Spanish padres, earthquakes, home some day.

(Nightmares still. Coming back from class and finding the empty house in Newark or Seattle or Portland. Searching for the family on the road to San Francisco. Finding them in the hall of mirrors, endless, beginningless mirrors at Palisades Park.)

Susan often imagined herself in San Francisco, living in one of those Victorian North Beach apartments, working by a bay window overlooking the Golden Gate, going out to browse at City Lights or to drink coffee at Café Trieste. But she still lived in Berkeley, tucked in a small apartment on the north side of the Cal campus. She had a good view of the city from her back window when the Acacia wasn't in bloom.

She climbed Hearst, enjoying the cold stillness. They told her not to walk at night. As a rape crisis volunteer, she knew more than statistics. But she could not lock herself up to protect her freedom. She needed this nighttime solitude, this stillness. Nothing but clear winter and the city across the water. Winter, with its survival course of contemplation and work, enlarged her. She cherished the grey, the constant steel grey. San Francisco grey. She had read Thomas Wolfe and had gone to Britain, but the London fog was shadowy rather than grey.

Susan understood now that something was intrinsically wrong with the last chapter. Sometimes you had to destroy to create, right? It takes courage to admit you've failed. The piece was too cognitive. It said what she thought, but had no emotional integrity. Perhaps she would have to begin all over again.

Susan was good at beginnings. "Engagé," as her mother's friend who read Lillian Hellman would say. Everyone envied Susan's drive and energy. Everyone said she would make it one day, because she knew what she wanted. And she had already had some success with her writing. While her friends opted for money or prestige or marriage, Susan had, as Judy admiringly put it, "sanitized herself of sexist, capitalist compromises." She was free of wifery, motherhood, careerism. She was free. That's the way they saw it. Free to get on with it.

She let the empty bus trundle past her. Tonight she wouldn't be encapsuled. That was why she left the party. It hadn't been any different than most. The music, in fact, had been very good. But she hated how Judy flirted with that Englishman. Perhaps Judy hadn't done anything except sit down next to him. No, it was the *way* Judy sat that bothered Susan. Just as it was the way Judy spoke. They had very different ways. In the end, she let Judy have her way. And she went on hers.

(No, Guy, it's nothing you've done. I just can't continue to be Professor Thompson's wife. Not your fault. Not anyone's fault.)

Susan knew she had to stop procrastinating. She just wasn't concentrating on the book. It had been due three weeks ago. But she had been paralyzed. She had always met deadlines before. Lately, though, she had regressed into this childhood

172

where she refused to work, where she waited for someone to motivate her, challenge her, cajole, scold. The punishment she managed herself: guilt was a ubiquitous noose.

She pushed open the door and switched on the light. She felt the cold immediately, realizing that she had been walking all the way with her coat open. She enjoyed working here in this office and having her apartment upstairs. In the evenings, she used to have friends over for coffee or hold meetings of the Left Caucus or the Rape Crisis Group. But she hadn't invited anyone since December, two months ago. She had started sleeping in the office. She had to finish the bloody book. She had thought that spending time with it would help. She couldn't give up an important project like this. Susan plugged in the electric heater, turned on the kettle, and dismissed her mother's warnings about conflagration as she made her way up to the freezing bathroom.

The heat still hadn't stretched across the room when she returned, so she stood by the electric fire, warming her hands on the cracking green elephant mug of tea. She should throw away this mug. Cracks cultivated germs. Besides, someday the thing would split in her hands. It was a kind of trophy, though, Professor Ash's mug. Her writing had such control, he said. She was a fine student, but he didn't want to give her any false hopes. Most girls chose a practical program like research or teaching.

She looked at the typewriter, hulking under its dark cover like a Lenten statue. What was she waiting for? She pulled away the cover and read the half page she had produced that afternoon. The direction seemed OK. All she needed to do was summarize a few points and conclude. No, she didn't know what it was, but something was terribly wrong.

She turned away again, opening the window for fresh air and looked across the Bay. She couldn't see through the fog to the city's skyline. A low cloud ceiling suspended Berkeley in the light night, as though under a private moon. Next to the window hung her own resin relief of a window—glossy green and orange irony. And next to that, a stream of magicians' scarves she had brought back from India. She liked the room; the shelf of Victorian novels, the postcards of workers she had picked up at the galleries. She felt reassured, as natural as one might feel in a personal shrine.

Susan flipped through the last pages of her previous chapter. So hard to end this book, hard to describe what happened to Marya Terazinya, hard to explain why she had wanted to write a biography of the Russian pianist. Marya Terazinya haunted her. It was Susan's own fault. She had single-mindedly sought out the woman after that night of Saint-Saëns at the Albert Hall. Susan hunted all over London for the faint Soviet recording of Marya's concerto. She found herself leafing through music journals on Charing Cross Road, anxious for the slightest mention of the obscure musician. Marya was young, ascetic, had no time for anything but her music. She lived in a Moscow bedsit with her piano. Susan admired the spare, accomplished life and planned to get an assignment to interview her. But one night, ten thousand miles away in a yesterday that was still today in the objectivity of international time treaties, Susan heard that Marya Terazinya was dead. A heart attack, according to *Pravda*. No further details. Only time crosses such borders easily. Would that it were so easy to cross time.

Susan had tried everything to finish the book: taping the chapters; reading parts aloud to friends; breaking her routine. Last week she had gone to a Russian art exhibit at the de Young Museum over in Golden Gate Park.

The park had been shrouded in the mist of February, cold and deserted, except for a few winos biding time between open hours at the missions. And a mother with her little daughter. Twinges of loss. Familiar sensations, but no memories surely. The only walks she ever took with her own mother were around shopping centers. Once she had seen a television program (she must have been eight or nine) of a family hiking through dry birch leaves. She remembered vowing that she would take her children for walks in the park. Her daughter and son. She had married Guy for a daughter and a son.

(She woke up asking how long it would take.
"Don't worry, Mrs. Thompson, a D and C is a simple
procedure."
Did he say no muss, no fuss?
"We'll have the tissue removed in twenty minutes. Good
thing you didn't wait longer."
"Honest, I can't have a baby now. Someday. But now
there's too much. . . ."
"Relax and count backwards with me now. Nine-eight-
seven. . . ."
Rustling leaves. Little girl.
"That's it dear, think pleasant thoughts. That's natural."
"I am a natural woman."
"Don't try to talk now, dear. Think about the girl
rustling."
"A girl, how can you tell?"
"About yourself, as a little girl, rustling."
Rustling like the taffeta of nuns' slips. Nuns don't have
children either. Everyone is their child. We are all God's
children. Thou shalt not kill.
"A simple procedure."
Extreme unction by nitrous oxide.
"Susan, it was an operation, after all. You're supposed to
be resting. Put down the notebook for a while."
"A simple procedure, Mrs. Thompson.")

That day in the park became a blank. She returned to the same place. They called it bronchitis, an impossible love affair, a severe depression. But Susan knew what the problem was: her will had run down. Maybe she should start the biography all over again. She had thrown away parts of her life before.

KASM buzzed surrender to Saturday night. Two-thirty. How long had she been phased out, oblivious to the high-pitched seething of the radio? She had done this so often lately, lost concentration, consciousness. She would find herself frozen for minutes, asleep, numb, paralyzed. Euthanasia should be legalized for those without brainwaves. She

175

swished the dial for company, for the speedy-dosey mono-
logues of adolescent DJ's who giggle to themselves through
the night.

*("Ms. Campbell, the editors have discussed it and much
as we respect your application, much as we acknowledge
your talent, we don't find your work acceptable. It's a
matter of, well, taking direction. Any magazine depends
on cooperation. Perhaps we were wrong to try out a
woman in this rather, uh, comradely ambience. And
perhaps, ultimately, you are an individualist. Perhaps
you should continue free-lance work. It's a question of
personality, really.")*

Susan welcomed the electronic scapeghosts. Inane pop music was a safe outlet for her anger. It was either them or her.
Or her work. After all this struggling, passionate as it was in
feminist terms, what did she have? A parable for her friends'
daughters? A reputation? What was that but a mortgage on
future work?

The time she wasn't writing, she should have been writing.
Borrowed hollows of time. When she couldn't write, she
couldn't edit and she couldn't socialize. The integrated contemporary woman, disintegrated. Suffocated by other people's
respect. Tired, chilled and alone in a drafty old office with an
expensive electric typewriter. She examined her incomplete
sentences with the close cruelty of a middle-aged woman
counting her wrinkles in a mirror. Maybe she should go back
to magazine articles. They paid well and provided a comfortable competence. The articles were mediocre, perhaps, but at
least they didn't make her feel like an imposter.

No. No. She just wasn't concentrating. She switched off
the radio and lifted the top of her stereo, irritated to find she
had forgotten to put away two records. The first one plopped
down and the room was possessed by a loud, brassy voice.
"Bill Bailey, wontya. . . ." How Susan hated that song. It
was a pre-feminist objection, recalling those Ed Sullivan Sunday nights. The fat, blonde woman in a sequinned gown bel-
lowed for forgiveness and then there would be "a really big

hand for Sandy Samone." Susan remembered her mother leaning heavier on the iron, looking from the flickering screen to her husband. "Right, I'll pay the rent when we get a place. Just you get us to San Francisco, Andy."

(When she heard that Sandy Samone was playing live at Dennyman's Piano Bar, Susan drove thirty miles to San Jose to hear her. Sandy Samone was older now. Blonder. But the voice was the same, the same mellow mediocrity, despite the fifth screwdriver. Susan sent her a drink and asked the barman to say it was from "an admirer."

Of course Sandy Samone wouldn't know Marya Terazinya. Not to be elitist, but there was a difference between Marya's art and Sandy's entertainment. Well, who survived, tell me that?

Who survived? Not on obscure discs between thin blue Soviet cardboard, but in real, voluptuous flesh and blood. "I know I done you wrong." Sandy made no precious attempt to transcend the suffering. She just kept pouring on the peroxide and singing. That's it, honey, swing it. "Mea culpa." Tell me who's laughing now. And what's the difference between crying and laughing? Maybe "ni kulturni," baby, but who survived?

And who has guys driving all the way from Stockton to see her? So what if the sets weren't as elaborate as they used to be—Marya Terazinya forgive her—she still had body and soul. Anyway, who noticed after six screwdrivers? What a treat. Admirers after all these years.)

Susan was not concentrating. A red light said the records she had not heard were over. OK, she knew it was ridiculous to romanticize Marya, the isolated artist, and Sandy, the passionate hack. It was even more ridiculous to have delusions of her grandeur or despair, to believe she had to become one or the other. Something was certain. Susan was a coward compared to Sandy Samone. Susan knew she would have swallowed the peroxide.

She could maintain no distance from the naked typewriter and the ream of blank bond paper. Susan felt she was tottering from adolescence to menopause, in a coma of glandular fever. Weren't there ages of relative sanity inbetween? The book was too long. Too didactic. Her friends in the CP would hate it. A lot of feminists would say it was too social- ist. And, finally, she knew, it was too badly written.

("Tell our listeners, Susan Campbell, to what do you attribute your drive? How did you survive female socialization?"

"Survive?" asked Susan.

"Yes, how did you survive the stereotyped condition- ing?" said the DJ. "Many of the women in our audience are undoubtedly wondering how you did it."

"Georges Sand decided at 27 that she was either going to be sane or crazy," said Susan.

"Perhaps we should go to a more specific question."

"Don't you see, it's all a choice?" said Susan. "To be mediocre or to take the risk."

"Yes, hmmmm, well, if we could return to your writing," he suggested patiently. "How did you determine your political, aesthetic and personal priorities?"

"You don't get it," she was growing more desperate. "It's all a choice, not to separate thought and feeling and action. That's what aesthetics and survival mean. You don't get it, do you, Mr. Interviewer?"

"Susan, let's get off the stage now," a friend materialized. "You really do need a rest. Let's get away for a while. Don't worry. It's only a taped show. Only a few women in the audience. Only a few women.")

"Damn telephone," Susan turned off the typewriter and walked over to answer it. "Damn telephone at four o'clock in the bloody morning. You're never completely free."

"Susan Campbell. Yes, this is Susan Campbell. Rape Crisis? Yes. Yes. Put her through now."

"When did it happen and are you OK?"

"How do you feel now?"

"No, it's not your fault. Get that idea out of your head right away."

"So you're going to believe someone who assaulted you in the street? He does have an interest in telling you it's your fault."

"That's it, cry if you want."

"And get angry if you want."

"Do you have any friends you can call?"

"Of course she'll understand."

"Not the end, yes, that's right."

"You can't undo it, no, but you don't have to *continue* being a victim."

"Sure, sure, cry if you want."

"Yes?"

"Of course I want to come to the police station with you."

"Don't apologize. We've all got to stop apologizing."

"Yes, certainly you should report it—for your own peace and for other women. You don't want him to do it again. A lot of us. . . ."

"To more of us that you imagine."

"Look, why don't I just come over and we can have some coffee?"

"No, no, love, I can't make you go. I don't want to make you."

"Why don't you just give me your number and I'll ring you later to see how you're feeling. . . ."

"Sure, it's your decision. It's up to. . . ."

Click. Nothing to do but wait now. People panic and think everyone is their enemy. Nothing to do but wait.

Susan went back to work. You know, perhaps it wasn't so thoroughly bad. Maybe it was her critique that was too cognitive rather than the writing itself. She had evaluated each word until she no longer saw a book or a chapter, but a chart of detailed decisions, one complicating the other. It was like being trapped in an algebra exam, having forgotten how to add minus numbers. Maybe she should have faith in the first idea; maybe she should just get on with it.

The introduction to this last chapter was right. And she had all the material. It was a matter of what came next. Of continuing. She turned on the typewriter and continued the paragraph. (Will. Incentive. Momentum. She was fond of litanies. Faith. She recalled the conversations with Sara on the train and on their wonderful visits since then. Faith.) The book would not resist change. It moved to the skill in her fingers. What mattered was the doing, not the planning or the worrying or the stupid apologizing. It didn't all have to be such a struggle.

Struggle. Where was the sisterhood now? Susan wondered sometimes if feminism was the ultimate in female masochism because there seemed to be nothing beyond the struggle. She had been retained as a good fighter, a prolific petitioner. Now, brittle with fatigue, she contemplated how she gave her loneliness to group consciousness, her anger to organized protest, her oppression to revolutionary retribution. So what if she were free from sexist family, teachers, husband, boss, critics? What was salvation if there was no afterlife?

She was free from all that, free for. . . .

She continued to type. For a moment, she did not know why. The book would not be perfect. It might not be very good. And it didn't keep her warm at night. This humming hulk slept under a different sheet. No, writing was not like making love or giving birth. The work, alone, was not enough. But it was the largest part of her whole. Her breathing eased with this understanding. Writing sustained her like nothing else. And accepting that, there was no possible conclusion except to continue.

◇

"Telephone. Finally." The low pitched ring continued as she lifted the receiver. She reached over and flicked off her travel alarm clock. Seven o'clock.

Susan drew the curtains and she was disappointed that the city was fogged in even more than the night before. There was usually some break at sunrise. The temperature must have dropped ten degrees because frost edged the window panes. Susan switched on the kettle and turned back to work.

Sisterhood

Pat walked along the sidewalk, looking up. Only one cell of Montreal Police Station Numéro Cinq seemed to be occupied. She saw the figure of a bulky young man, straight brown hair straggling to the collar of the beige sports jacket. It could have been an alcoholic hard-hat or a thug, maybe a plainclothes policeman off duty. But Pat knew it was her sister Rosemary. Rosemary, hunched and tense, trying to ignore the smell of the horse-shit from the stable and the rattling of the poker chips upstairs. Rosemary reading or writing one of her Marxist texts.

Pat remembered Rosemary running up these slippery grey steps when they were kids, playing tag on the way home from St. Paul's. No one dared follow. She had warned Rosemary, twenty-five years ago, that she would get locked up if she kept behaving like *that*.

"Ms. Jordan, please."

"Upstairs, lady, in the Bridal Suite."

Pat winced, less irritated by the sergeant's sarcasm than by what it predicted about Rosemary's mood. By now she should be used to the effect of her sister's tempers on the rest of humanity.

She had defended Rosemary's right to play football. Gradually she, too, became keen on sports and followed Rosemary's progress with a fine track record of her own. Pat had explained to their parents why Rosemary wanted to divorce the American draft resister three years after she had explained why Rosemary wanted to marry him. And that had decided Pat, herself, against wifery.

"Ms. Jordan," she said, slurring the "Ms." and hating herself for lacking Rosemary's strength. "Ms." was simple enough: why did she pretend to be slurring "Miss" or "Mrs."? The West Indian guard considered her with remote curiosity. Not the usual sort of visitor, she supposed he was thinking, not like Rosemary's ragged radical friends in their $50 hiking boots. She looked like a "proper doc," still in her respectable clothes. She knew Rosemary would hate the pantyhose. They always got into a godalmighty row about them causing yeast infections. Rosemary giving *her* medical advice.

But then, they had always been collaborators. At least she had always collaborated in Rosemary's schemes. In some ways, Rosemary had been the classic older sister. All Pat had to do was follow the red-splattered road. When Pat played Saint Joan in high school, she just played Rosemary. However, their parents always recognized that Pat was the sensible one, the accomplished one. Graduating at the top of her medical class. Even Rosemary accepted her bourgeois credentials when Pat started teaching a self-examination course for women.   *

Pat could smell the horseshit as she approached the south corridor. She recalled her panic, years ago, when Rosemary said she was going to steal one of the horses. They were on their way home from a novena. She dared Rosemary to go ahead and promised to come along for the ride if she smuggled the mare.

"Bitch." The guard's voice carried down the corridor. "Just watchit, bitch."

Pat tried to ignore the shouting by listening to the quick clacking of her platform heels on the linoleum floor.

"I'm Dr. Jordan." She heard herself assuming the propriety that Rosemary detested. And she saw it disarm the guard.

"I would like to see my sister."

XIV
Rondo

The waiter carried a piece of Larry Blake's special angel food cake to the next table and placed it in front of the jock in the pin-striped shirt. Susan regarded her own diluted Coke and wondered how much longer she would wait for Guy. She wanted to order a coffee, but then she wouldn't have enough money for bus fare home. It was true that she was going to get an advance for the book. She would only have to wait a while longer. So here she was, ten years out of college and still counting her pennies for coffee while the varsity champ was swallowing the restaurant whole.

"Hello, excuse me, but are you Susan Campbell?"

Susan regarded a girl in jeans and a Mexican flowered blouse. Of course she wasn't a girl; she was a college student, a young woman. Susan would be offended if some man were to call her a girl. But in looking at her and in looking at herself, this stranger seemed a girl. Susan realized that the girl must be paging her for Guy. At least, she thought, he was courteous enough to try and reach me.

"Yes," she said at last. "I'm Susan Campbell."

"I'm very pleased to meet you," said the girl shyly. "I'm Debbie Guthrie and I wanted to thank you for that talk you gave about Marya Terazinya and your book last week."

Susan tried to hide her disappointment with a late and crooked smile.

The young woman considered her closely, as if she were inspecting for forgery. "When you spoke at Dwinelle Hall last

Friday," she said and then looked embarrassed at having to remind Susan of her own lecture. "I was particularly struck by what you said about fiction overlapping with biography, about art and politics."

"Won't you sit down?" asked Susan, hoping that the stranger (Now she had a name. What was it? Debbie, of course. But it was too late to say, "Won't you sit down, Debbie?") would leave so she could save her coffee money. Susan realized she was too tired to walk home. Where the hell was Guy?

"Well, I wouldn't want to impose," said Debbie, as she slid nimbly into the booth. "But when I first noticed you over here, the waiter said you were expecting someone. When they didn't show up after all this time, I thought you might like the company."

Silence.

Debbie was frowning now. She seemed to be recalling just what she had said, checking that all the words came out in order.

"Who knows," said Susan, truly confused, herself, about whether she was being polite or masochistic or maternal. "Maybe I was waiting for you."

Debbie stuttered, "I, I, I mean I just wanted to pay my respects."

At this they both laughed. The younger woman looked more comfortable.

"If you really don't mind the company," said Debbie, "I'll join you for a cup of coffee."

A little overwhelmed by all this energy, Susan signaled the waiter to bring two coffees, hoping desperately that Debbie had enough money to pay for her own. Or perhaps Guy would show up and loan her money to pay for both of them.

She was pretty, Susan noticed, with those coils of red black hair curled around her clear, moon face. She had that innocent, natural chic which Revlon was selling now. However, Debbie was the genuine article. She had saved herself so much time not using mascara. She had saved herself whole days, perhaps weeks, in her freedom from buying and applying and removing make-up. But then, Susan couldn't blame herself for the eye shadow in her own history. Everyone used it then. Maybelline made you visible. Guy might not have noticed her otherwise. Susan had stopped wearing it in England, not out of ideology, but for vanity. The mascara had made grey dabs on her cheeks (worse with midnight blue), scars from this new, damp climate. When she first looked in the mirror with naked eyes, she seemed younger. But Susan doubted that she had ever looked as young as her present companion. Forgetting fatigue, Susan wondered what she might learn from this younger person.

Debbie was talking rapidly, nervously. "I've always admired your work. And from what I could discern, your whole approach to life."

Susan nodded uneasily.

"You see, I want to write," said Debbie. "I do write. I have fourteen notebooks of journal. I think the journal is becoming a genre in its own right. Don't you think so?"

Embarrassed by such admiration, Susan was also scared that if she accepted it, she would be caught in a charade. She had had these chats with younger women before and they left her uncomfortable for hours afterward.

"Well, I liked *Journal of A Solitude*," said Susan simply. Maybe if she sounded dull enough, Debbie would just go away. Then, ashamed of her coldness, Susan realized how disappointed and angry she was that Guy had not shown up. Just another element of the familiar suspense that played between them. Would they cross the border? Would that fucker ever get to Phoenix? Susan smiled at the memory of their escape to Canada, at the other borders they had crossed. How many were left?

Debbie smiled. "*Journal of A Solitude,* oh yes," she agreed and followed with a rapturous critique of May Sarton. Then Debbie told her breathlessly that she was in her last term at Berkeley, majoring in English literature, caught between graduate school and just getting on with her writing. Did Susan ever have to make that choice?

Susan remembered how she used to give oral resumes like

this, detailing what she presumed to be her accomplishments as well as her current insights and questions, so the other person would think her worthy of attention. At that time, life seemed to be a set of necessary hurdles, the passing of which granted you some kind of wisdom.

"I've done OK in the writing classes here," Debbie continued. "But what does that tell me? All the professors are men. I'm really committed to the development of matriarchal language. Like what Mary Daly's doing."

Susan felt a twinge of rivalry when Debbie mentioned Mary Daly. This dissolved as she continued listening.

She was listening not so much to content as to pattern. Lately this had happened to her often: she was claimed by students, asked for advice, and then presented with their autobiographies.

"This may sound stupid," Debbie began to say as she twisted the long chain of seed beads which hung from her neck. (Weren't they out of style now, these three-foot strands? Susan thought about her own Brazilian beads and wondered whether students were still as careful to get their jewelry from the correct political groups. Well, at least Debbie wasn't one of these punk rockers with safety pins in her cheeks.) "Don't worry about sounding stupid," Susan said kindly.

Debbie still looked concerned. Susan wanted to reach out and say, "It's OK, love." But she didn't know what "it" was. She could not figure out what the other woman wanted from her.

"Well," said Debbie, "do you *like* writing? I mean last week you described it as painful. So *why* do you do it?"

"There is no *why*," said Susan, surprised at the swift sureness of her answer. "*How* was always the problem. *How* was I going to pay the rent? *How* was I going to afford the beans? *How* was I going to find the courage and perseverance to keep writing when people weren't publishing my books?"

This all sounded rather grand, Susan recognized, a bit abstract. But she had never asked herself why. Now she felt like a phony, playing Jane Fonda, playing Lillian Hellman.

Was it a mortal sin to impersonate a writer?

"Yes, I do like writing," she finally answered the question.

Debbie was astonishingly familiar with Susan's work. She asked questions about articles Susan had forgotten. Almost forgotten. Debbie was full of questions. Do you work early in the morning? A set number of hours a day? Debbie wasn't so much interested in how to find the courage to write as she was in how to publish any or all of her fourteen journals. This made sense to Susan.

"But you'll need a job to support yourself," said Susan. "Something to pay the rent."

"There's family money," said Debbie. "I'm sure I could get a loan from my parents."

Family money, thought Susan, staring down at the empty Coke glass to hide her—what was it—her anger, jealousy, sense of unfairness. How much easier it would have been for her if she had had money or encouragement or even interest from her family. Was it fair? Ridiculous question, Susan realized, swallowing the resentment. Debbie did not determine her own pedigree. Fairness was a belief she should have left behind in Catholic school. Was it fair that Mohammed had to stay in Agadir to support his family? Was it fair that Alexander died of bronchitis in a damp London flat so far from the warmth of Zimbabwe? Was it fair that her own mother still worked at age seventy in a downtown diner? No, life was not fair. Life was making the most of what you had—persuading envy into generosity and guilt into compassion. There was enough of the world to go around.

"We used your Celtic book in my ethnic relations course," Debbie said. "I would love to go to Ireland and write journals. That's where my grandmother is from. How do you feel about the Celtic work now?"

Susan was torn between talking about her research and just making an excuse to leave. But the damn waiter hadn't even brought the coffee yet. So she told Debbie about the Cornish work, about that dreadful winter afternoon on the cliffs, about Ronald's death, about the dwindling correspondence from Andre and Colin.

"Why did you go to London?" Debbie demanded abruptly. The urgency held Susan closely, as if Debbie were trying to photograph some illusive self image. In focusing the camera, however, Debbie would have to notice that the background was a mirror which would reflect both of them. Whatever came out of this talk wouldn't be a portrait of a role model but a photo of the two of them together. And Susan doubted that Debbie's depth of field was large enough to get them both in focus.

Susan answered that she had hoped moving to England would end the boredom and guilt and pain of her marriage. It was the *beginning* for which she wasn't prepared. The mitosis. One cannot control growth. (If she couldn't control her own, how could she help Debbie, she wondered. No, she stopped herself. Debbie hadn't asked for help.)

Debbie said she often thought about giving up men altogether, but right now she was relating to a good, non-sexist guy. "I'll stay as long as it's not oppressive."

"Good luck," Susan said, holding back to protect Debbie from her sarcasm, to protect herself from her confusion. Should Susan explain that she still liked sleeping with men? That she hated waking next to them, hated the heavy emptiness of the mornings after? Still, she did wish Debbie luck. Perhaps this new generation of men would be different, perhaps.

Debbie grasped the silence anxiously, "You know what really bothers me about the writing is that I wonder if it's a substitute. Maybe I'm putting all my creative energies into literature when I should be having a family."

Susan looked stunned. Debbie reached over and reassuringly patted her hand.

"Oh, I don't mean a patriarchal nuclear explosion family," said Debbie. "I mean a growing relationship that offers personal affirmation. Sometimes I think about the writing, in comparison, as empty."

Susan thought about how work had filled her life. She thought about the hours she stole from her paid job in order to finish the book. She shook her head in exhaustion, incomprehension. For the first time this afternoon, Debbie seemed to notice that Susan wasn't impermeable.

"Listen, friend," Susan said, "I wish I had these answers—for me as well as for you. But I don't know. I don't know if I have time for children. I don't know whether I'll be with a man or a woman. Choices. Freedom just leads to more damn choices."

"Well, I think we can have both," Debbie said encouragingly, "love and work."

"I hope so," Susan laughed, feeling relaxed now and quite certain of her fondness for this kid.

Debbie looked at her watch. "I should be going." She sounded both relieved and sad.

Susan considered the time. No, Guy would not be coming today. Would they ever cross the border?

"Which way are you headed?" Susan brightened.

"Actually, I'm half-an-hour late to a class on Victorian prose in Le Conte Hall," said Debbie.

"I'm walking that way, too," said Susan, putting down the last coins from her purse as a tip.

The two women threaded their way through the stands and shoppers on Telegraph Avenue. Debbie pumped Susan with questions about the sixties, about People's Park, anti-war marches, the Panthers. Susan told Debbie that she was setting the revolution in the wrong decade.

"Maybe the choices were posed in the sixties," said Susan. "But it was living through those choices, that was the sticky part. And that happened later on, in the seventies, in the eighties."

"But you're working through them," said Debbie, nervous that she had somehow made the older woman vulnerable, forcibly exposing her to her own past. "You survived."

"Survived," said Susan, thinking of Sandy Samone and Marya Terazinya. "Oh, I think so. More than survived."

Debbie smiled and continued smiling as Susan talked about how Berkeley had survived. Telegraph carried the same seedy excitement, some of the same people. The blustering evangelist, old Hubert, had weathered the scorn of hippies and was now a venerable figure to the squads of clean kids who called themselves "just Christians." The tall man whose face was long ago eaten in some tragic chemistry experiment looked at Susan skeptically when she smiled at him. She wondered if he had remembered her timid smiles from ten years before. The Bubble Lady Poet wore the same ragged pigtail and the same ragged black coat. Maybe she was afraid that without them, tourists wouldn't recognize her from the People's Park mural.

And it did not matter that some of her memories were lost to fiction, Susan told herself. The pursuit of art was more worthy than the pursuit of nostalgia. Whenever Susan visited the campus, she preferred to go as a ghost.

Debbie did not believe in ghosts. She believed in legend rather than timelessness. She was interested in Susan's past only in so far as it related to their present. How had Susan planned her life? Debbie wanted to know. When Susan was a student, what did she expect to become?

"You mean, what did I think I'd be doing now?" asked Susan.

"Yes," said Debbie. "I mean did you think you would have traveled and done these things and then moved back here and that you would be a writer?"

Susan had to admit that the scenario had gone something like that. She had to admit that she was no longer the earnest student or the novice writer and that she had no right to many of her doubts, even if she wasn't comfortable with success. Susan did not want to materialize, but she remembered Debbie did not believe in ghosts. And for this, she resented Debbie a little. She felt like the native, who finding her home settled by immigrants, must ultimately admit that everyone is an immigrant. For Debbie, there was no past that was not history.

As they reached the edge of campus, Debbie said, "My house had a 1968 party last week."

"A what?" Susan asked, incredulous, although she knew one day the sixties would be processed into nostalgia chic. "Why?"

"To celebrate the anniversary of the Open Speech Movement," Debbie said.

"You mean the Free Speech Movement," said Susan.

"The sad thing was," Debbie continued deadpan, "no one knew what to wear."

"What to wear?" Susan repeated numbly.

"You know," said Debbie, "what gear you guys wore in those days. None of the kids are much into politics. I think I looked pretty realistic. I found some heavy boots and a black armband . . . . You wouldn't like to meet them?" Debbie asked tentatively. "The people in my house, I mean."

Susan nodded.

"Supper sometime?"

"I'd be delighted," said Susan.

At Ludwig's Fountain, they both laughed at the three dogs chasing each other's tails. They stopped at several of the propaganda tables which were lined all the way to Sather Gate. A young man in a yarmulke was arguing furiously with two Jews for Jesus. A fiddler was getting the excess attention playing some West Virginia song that, strangely, half the crowd seemed to know.

"Were Fridays like this in your day?" asked Debbie.

"Well, give or take a few bayonets and billy clubs. Yes, I guess when the tear gas settled, some Fridays were very much like this, especially in the early spring. Now look at that pink in the petals there. You know, it was Professor Riley's Victorian prose class that made me want to go to England."

"Oh, yeah," said Debbie. "He was driving people away even then?"

Susan smiled at the younger woman and thought it was a very perfect Friday, past and present.

Betty Medsger

ABOUT THE AUTHOR

Valerie Miner is a widely published novelist, journalist and critic. As a political activist, she is committed to the development of a strong international women's movement.

Her novels reflect concerns and challenges of contemporary women. BLOOD SISTERS is about working class Irish women and the IRA. MIRROR IMAGES describes the climate of sexual harassment and rape on an American campus. She is coauthor of TALES I TELL MY MOTHER and HER OWN WOMAN. Her fiction and journalism have appeared in *Sinister Wisdom, Saturday Review, Ms., The New Statesman, Spare Rib, The Economist, Saturday Night* and other periodicals. She teaches in The Field Studies Program at U.C. Berkeley.